GIVE ME FOREVER

LAYLA HAGEN

1

SAM

"I think she looks a lot like Travis," Gran exclaimed, cooing over the newborn.

My brother Travis became a father last night. As a pediatrician at the hospital, I checked in on my niece right after she was born. Luckily, I was on shift when my sister-in-law's water broke, and my brother rushed her right in. The dude was a basket case, which would've been funny if I didn't feel sorry for him. I'd seen lots of dads lose their cool when their first baby was born. They wanted to do everything right, as did my brother, but at the same time felt so helpless throughout it all. Dr. Johnson performed the delivery, and I was there to give Travis moral support afterward.

Currently, I was keeping a close eye on Bonnie, Travis's wife. She was happy but tired, which was to be expected. Our gran and parents were overwhelming her, and I was completely surprised that my brothers and their better halves hadn't shown up too. I'd cautioned them that the new parents needed rest, but I'd expected them to completely ignore me. I was glad they didn't.

"Everyone, come on, out of here. You've had enough visitation time. Let them rest," I said.

"Nonsense," Gran said. "Everyone else can go. I'll stay here and rock this sweet girl to sleep."

She seemed unable to take her eyes off the baby.

I cleared my throat, using my stern doctor voice. "No, Gran. It's best if we leave them alone. The baby will fall asleep anyway, and Bonnie also needs to rest."

Gran looked at me severely. "Young man, don't think you can tell me what to do just because you have a doctor's coat on."

I grinned. "Yes, I can."

"Beatrice, come on," Mom said. "He's right. Bonnie needs rest."

Bonnie smiled sheepishly. "Beatrice, I promise that once we're home, you can come visit as much as you want. But now we're all exhausted."

At once, my grandmother's demeanor changed. She blinked, nodding before returning the baby to Bonnie's arms.

I was grateful that she was at least listening to Bonnie.

I knew this was a momentous day for both my grandmother and my parents. It was only the second grandchild in the Maxwell family. Even though there were six of us brothers, along with two very close cousins, only my brother Tate who had a daughter.

"It's been a while since we've had a baby in the family," Mom said, as if reading my thoughts. Paisley, Tate's daughter, was a teenager. He was about to have a second kid soon.

Boy, time flies.

"No problem, Mom. We're happy you stopped by. Come on, I'll walk out with you," Travis said.

Taking the now-sleeping baby from Bonnie's arms, he put her in the crib next to the bed. Bonnie instantly fell asleep, and we all walked out as quietly as possible from the room.

Once Travis closed the door behind him, Mom exploded. "Oh, she's so pretty. I wanted to snuggle her the whole time, but Beatrice hogged her."

The look on Gran's face was priceless as she said, "It's my great-grandmother privilege."

Mom glanced at Travis. "I'm sorry we monopolized your time with Bonnie and the baby." She sounded truly apologetic. "We thought about waiting until you were home, but…"

"She considered it for maybe five seconds before deciding it was impossible," Dad interjected with a grin.

Travis chuckled. "It's all good. Bonnie is beyond happy that the family is embracing her like this. She's just tired."

My brother was right. Bonnie's mom was an insanely cold woman, so I could see how our family would be a welcome change.

Bonnie always seemed happy to be around the Maxwell clan, but I was going to advise her to take it easy with visits. The birthing went fine, but she needed to rest up here where people could help her. Once she got home, any relaxing with a newborn would go out the window.

"Listen, Sam, what's the policy on bringing your own food here? The breakfast we got sucked, and I want to spoil my woman," Travis said.

I waved him off. "Don't worry about it. I'll cover for you. Buy something delicious for you two to eat. The hospital food is nothing to brag about, but it could be worse. Speaking of food, do you all want to go to the cafeteria?"

"Are we keeping you from anything, son?" Dad asked.

"No, I took the shift last night, so I'm off today. I just wanted to hang around and see if Bonnie needed anything." But I was starved, too, and wouldn't mind a strong cup of coffee.

"All right, then. Let's go," Mom said as we all went downstairs.

The place was semifamiliar to me. It was only my second month here, as I'd recently relocated from Honduras. The cafeteria was full as always with patients and doctors milling around. As the group found a table, I bought coffees for everyone, and Dad bought muffins.

Once we joined them, Mom looked around, observing the layout. "This is a nice place. I'm so happy you decided to stay here and be close to home."

"I haven't signed a permanent contract yet," I reminded her carefully. I didn't want her to get her hopes up. I wasn't sure I was staying in Chicago for good. I was of half a mind to go back to Doctors Without Borders. I'd worked with them for years, gallivanting around the world, and it really had been a rewarding experience. I'd been in Central Africa before relocating to Honduras.

I'd come back to Chicago for Olivia—we'd been in a long-distance relationship for a while. I figured we could take things to the next level if I moved back here. Turned out she was seeing someone else behind my back. Yeah, I was bitter about it. I would eventually let it go, but not yet. The whole thing was too fresh in my mind.

The other reason I was here was because I was in talks with the CEO of the hospital to add a pro bono clinic. After my experience in Doctors Without Borders, it was something very important to me.

"Oh, honey, don't say that. We just got you back," Mom said. She knew what happened with Olivia—they all did—and although they were disappointed in her, my family was happy we didn't stay together. My brothers thought she wasn't that "into" me. They'd never met her because she'd always found excuses to ditch family gatherings, but they were spot-on, considering she was dating someone else.

"Careful, brother. Next thing you know, Mom and Gran will emotionally blackmail the rest of us to convince you to stay," Travis said.

Mom straightened up. "Oh, we don't need you kids to do our dirty work. Beatrice and I are clever enough."

I chuckled. Damn, I'd been away for too long. I missed my

family a lot. We'd always been one for all and all for one, having one another's backs.

"Haven't you missed us at all?" Mom asked.

"I see. You really are going straight for the punch," I teased. "Of course I missed you. And I'm not saying I'll necessarily leave again. I just want you to keep in mind that everything's up in the air. I don't want you to get your hopes up."

"Hmm." Clearly she didn't agree with me. "Sam, have you thought about moving from Travis's hotel? You can't stay there forever."

"I'm looking for something else."

I heard Travis snicker and glared at him in warning. He knew my plan. I didn't want him to spill the beans. I was sure my family would have a lot of opinions, and I wasn't ready for them.

"That's great," Mom said, her eyes lighting up. That was her getting her hopes up. Now I felt like an ass.

While we finished our coffee, we spoke a bit about when Bonnie and the baby would be allowed to go home, and then my parents and my grandmother rose from the table.

"It's time for us to go. You tell us when we can come visit again," Mom said, looking at Travis, who glanced at me. He needed me to use my "doctor voice," as he called it.

"I don't think any more visits are necessary, Mom, because Bonnie's probably going home tomorrow," I explained. "You're all welcome to visit her then. For now, she needs rest."

Gran sighed dramatically. "Come on, let's go. We're not wanted here."

As soon as they were out of earshot, Travis chuckled. "Man, they're laying it on thick, aren't they?"

I shrugged. "You've got to give it to them. At least they did listen when Bonnie told them to leave."

"Why didn't you tell them you plan to move in with Avery?" He flashed me a shit-eating grin.

"Because then they would give me crap like you're about to do. And besides, that's not set in stone either."

Avery Sinclair had been my girlfriend during high school. Our relationship ended abruptly after prom, and I hadn't seen her since. Our high school had set up an alumni Facebook group, and someone posted about a loft that was available. We were both interested in it, but she needed someone to share it with her. The rent was high, and the loft itself was huge. I could afford it myself, and I didn't need a roommate, but I thought I'd help her out.

I'd told Travis last night after I saw the Facebook post. He'd given me shit then and clearly still wasn't done with it.

"Just saying, I think it's a bad idea. And if the family knew, they would tell you the exact same thing."

I smiled lazily. "See? That's why I don't ask their opinions. I don't need anyone to tell me I'm wrong."

"Spoken like a true doctor," he said, rolling his eyes. "You're playing with fire."

I wasn't. He was ridiculous. Avery and I had broken up more than ten years ago. Besides, there would be very little actual "living together." I worked crazy hours, so I'd be at the hospital more than at the loft.

"Man, you can't lie to me," Travis said. "Check out that look on your face. You want to see Avery again."

"Why not? I'm sure it's going to be interesting to catch up."

"Hah! 'Catch up.' I'd make a bet, but there's no one here to bet with."

"You all are still betting?" I asked. My siblings and cousins started this habit a long time ago. It used to be fun, but since now it was about me, I wasn't sure if I was thrilled.

"Only on special occasions."

"Why am I not part of that?"

"Because you told us you don't want to be part of the WhatsApp group. Remember, dickhead?"

That was true, but it had been for practical reasons. First, I'd been in a different time zone. And second, everyone texted *constantly* in that group. I couldn't keep up with it. At best I could check it only once a day, and by then it was overwhelming with over a hundred messages.

"I've always been the odd man out," I said.

"I agree," Travis agreed, and we laughed.

Almost everyone in my family went into business. My grandparents and parents had owned Maxwell Bookstores, a very successful chain of stores. They sold it many years ago, and each of my brothers had gone into business in one way or another. Tate owned wineries. Declan, the oldest, was a lawyer. Considering how much trouble anyone got into at any given time, it was good we had a lawyer in the family. Luke owned an architecture company. Both our cousins, Reese and Kimberly, worked with Travis in his hotel. Our brother Tyler was the only other odd man out like me. He was a pro hockey player.

I knew from an early age I wanted to be a doctor. It was my calling. I'd never regretted my choice.

I was the odd man out in another way too. I was the only single brother left. It was bizarre. When I left for Doctors Without Borders, all my brothers were single. Now they were all either engaged or married.

"You know what? I could ask everyone's opinion in our WhatsApp group," Travis suggested.

"You really want to broadcast this, don't you?" Man, he was such a smartass.

"Nah. It makes you uncomfortable, so I won't do it. But knowing our family, it's going to get out sooner rather than later."

"You and I are the only people who know. If it gets out, it's because you spilled the beans."

He grinned. "You know it."

I took out my phone and messaged Avery on Facebook. I'd wanted to see her again for years, but after she moved from

Chicago, we'd lost track of each other. For a long time, I didn't think she'd want me to contact her anyway.

Sam: Hey! It's been a while. Want to set up a time to visit the loft? Can't wait to catch up.

2

AVERY

"It still feels surreal to be back," I said as my best friend, Alana, held up her glass of wine. I clinked mine against hers.

"I'm glad to have my bestie back," she replied, taking a sip.

I looked around her small apartment. She'd been gracious enough to let me crash with her. When I called her a few weeks ago to tell her I was thinking about coming back to Chicago, she immediately offered me a place to live. I was camping out on her pullout couch in the living room. Although the bed was comfortable, and I enjoyed sharing her living space, I felt guilty for cramping her style.

"Don't! I know what you're thinking," Alana said.

I glanced back at her, putting my glass of wine on the dining room table. Cutting a slice of my chicken breast, I said quickly, "I'm not thinking anything."

"I know you. You might have been out of town for the past million years, but I still know that look on your face. You feel guilty."

"Fine, I do." I took a bite and chewed slowly, savoring it. We were enjoying dinner at home tonight.

"You can pay me back in jewelry."

I grinned. Since I was a jewelry designer, that was totally up my alley. "Will do. But I'm going to be out of your hair quickly, I promise."

"You have those two apartments lined up that you showed me yesterday, right?"

"Yeah, but honestly, I don't like either of them."

She wrinkled her nose, which transported me right back to high school. She'd had the exact same expression back then too. My God, it was surreal to be here. Everything was different but somehow also the same.

"I still have that loft that Sam is also interested in," I continued. Simply saying his name caused my stomach and the tips of my fingers to tingle. Sam had been my first boyfriend ever, and my first love, back in high school.

A couple days ago, I saw an announcement in the alumni Facebook group that someone was renting out a loft. It was gorgeous but far too expensive for me. It was a huge space for just one person anyway, so I told the renter I was interested but only to share. To my astonishment, Sam was interested in it as well.

For the life of me, I couldn't understand why he would even want a roommate. He could certainly afford the loft on his own. He was a Maxwell, after all.

"Sam Maxwell! Is he as fine as he was in high school?"

"I don't know. I haven't seen him since," I said. He'd missed the high school reunion a few years ago.

"I hear he's a renowned doctor. He's worked with Doctors Without Borders for years."

"That doesn't surprise me," I admitted. Sam had harbored that dream of working for the organization ever since we were in high school. I loved that about him; he was very caring that way. His family was well off, yet he wanted to break his back, studying and practicing medicine.

"You replied to Sam?"

"Not yet. I'll go look at the place again. I want to keep all my options open." Despite what my friend said, I didn't want to overstay my welcome. Besides, moving somewhere that I could call my own, even if it was a shared apartment, would be a step in the right direction to rebuilding my life.

Camping here on her couch felt temporary. It made me feel lost in limbo, like I was a teenager all over again.

But now I had a plan. First I was going to move into my own place. Then I was going to start building my business again from the ground up.

Pain fluttered in my chest at the thought of everything I'd lost, but that was what I got for trusting the wrong people.

"Do you want me to come with you to see the apartments?" Alana asked between bites. She'd cooked chicken parmigiana, and it was amazing.

In high school, both of us had barely known how to make grilled cheese sandwiches. But my friend had developed her culinary skills over the years, bringing them to an excellent level. Grilled cheese was still a staple in my diet.

"No, that's okay. The appointments are mostly at odd hours, and I don't want you to take time off at work." She was a curator at a local gallery.

"Let me know if you change your mind. I can act as a chaperone between you and Sam." Her devilish wink was hilarious.

I chuckled. "Oh, come on, Alana. Sam and I were together a lifetime ago." It felt that way, anyway. We'd probably grown into different people. I figured it would be the same as living with a stranger. I wondered if he was still as hot as in high school. If he was, that might complicate things a *tad*.

"If you say so. Let me just test this theory." She took out her phone, twirling a strand of her blonde hair around her fingertip. She'd been a knockout even in high school but wasn't part of the popular gang. The two of us had our own bookish corner back then. We weren't bullied or anything, just not part of the cool club. We never cared about it either. Alana and I called ourselves The Blondes because we had the same shade of dark-blonde shoulder-length hair, though she had blue eyes, and mine were green.

People often asked us if we were sisters because we looked alike. In fact, Alana looked more like me than my real sister. My younger sister, Jamie, took after Mom: she was brunette with dark brown eyes. I missed her and my mom tremendously. I wished they hadn't moved away from Chicago, but Jamie went to study in Maine and stayed there after graduation. Our mom moved to Miami, where she was originally from. She'd raised us on her own, fighting for everything tooth and nail. Mom deserved a great retirement, being around her childhood friends, maybe even dating a little. She was happy there, and that made my heart content. She'd always struggled in Chicago.

When we were kids, I remembered her often talking fondly about her childhood home. Once, I asked her why we didn't just move back. She said Jamie and I were at an excellent school that would set us up for the future, and that was true. We both had a scholarship at the elite private school where I met Sam and Alana. And Mom was right—it had opened a lot of doors. Jamie was a successful accountant now.

I, on the other hand, completely blew it. I took a chance on my business and on Sophia, my business partner—someone I'd considered a friend for years—and I'd made a mess of all of it. It didn't matter. I could build it all back up. I was going to find my way again. I felt it in my bones that it was a good idea to come back to Chicago. It was home to me.

"Here. Found him," Alana exclaimed. "Hot damn!"

I sat up straight in my chair. "What?" I asked her, holding my breath.

"Okay, I didn't think it was possible, but Sam looks even hotter than in high school."

"Impossible," I replied immediately. In my mind, I could conjure him up just as he was, even though I hadn't seen him in sixteen years. Dark hair, baby blue eyes, muscles that went on for days because he was on the lacrosse team, and a smile that would melt glaciers. You couldn't possibly beat perfection.

She turned the phone around, and I swallowed hard.

All right. I take it all back.

Grabbing the phone, I brought it closer and zoomed in on the picture. I first looked at his face. Somehow it was even more handsome than in high school. He'd been young then, but now he was a man through and through. The lines of his cheekbones were more angular. The smile was still absolutely panty melting. His dark hair was cropped short. And those blue eyes, well, hell. I zoomed out a bit, looking at his body from a bird's-eye view. He was wearing a shirt with short sleeves.

What kind of doctor had those kinds of muscles? This was insane.

"Are you rethinking my offer of chaperoning?" Alana asked on a laugh.

I gave her back the phone quickly. "No, not at all." My stomach was somersaulting.

"You little liar. You practically swallowed your tongue when I showed you the picture."

"The man is annoyingly, sinfully hot," I admitted. "I think I was just surprised because I hadn't seen him in so long."

I'd finished my chicken, so I focused on my wine instead. He didn't have his own picture as his profile on Facebook. I'd searched the other social sites earlier and didn't find him anywhere. Leave it to Alana to pull it up.

"It's a good thing you've shown me the picture, though," I told her. "Now I can brace myself."

"Oh, I don't know," Alana said. "If he turns up the charm, I don't think you stand a chance."

I sat up straighter. "Alana! I'm really not at the point in my life where I can think about anything except getting my shit together."

Her smile fell. "I'm sorry. I was just teasing you, thinking it might take your mind off everything."

I took my phone from the pocket of my jeans, bringing up my texts.

"I'm going to send him a message that I'll go see the apartment." I sent it quickly before I could change my mind. I couldn't lie—seeing that picture did things to me.

I didn't want to analyze those *things* too closely. It had been a long time, and I was sure we were different people with different priorities.

He replied right away.

Sam: Can't wait to see you, Avery.

I blushed as a few memories popped up in my mind.

"Is that a blush I'm seeing?" Alana asked.

I looked up from the phone. There was no hiding from her. It felt like no time had passed between us. Suddenly I wondered if it would feel the same way when I saw Sam—like I was still that eighteen-year-old who was sure he was the love of my life.

"Yep. I can't believe it."

"I'm sorry. I do have to tease you a bit more about it. I just can't help it."

That made me laugh. "That's fine. I think I've taken life too seriously lately."

Grabbing our glasses, we moved out onto her balcony. It was small, but it overlooked an inner courtyard that was surprisingly quiet. We sat down on the rattan chairs, clinking glasses again.

"Let's play a little game. How do you think things will play out when you see him?"

I bit my lip, thinking hard. "Well, he is clearly not the same guy I knew. He's even hotter."

"Do you think he'll flirt?"

He wouldn't do that, would he? Suddenly, I wasn't sure if this was a good idea. I didn't want to camp on Alana's couch for too long, but could I really live with Sam?

"I don't know. I think he might."

Alana grinned. "He still keeps you on your toes, huh?"

"Looks like it."

3

SAM

"Dr. Maxwell, is there anything else you need?" Nurse Christine asked me.

"No, thanks. I'm going to head out."

She nodded, and I left the exam room. First, I was going to stop by the doctors' lounge and grab a sandwich before leaving to see the apartment.

Being in a hospital still felt strange to me. I spent the first years of my stint with Doctors Without Borders in dangerous areas. It had been a stressful time but also very rewarding. I was making a difference, and I'd learned invaluable skills. A doctor always had to react well under pressure and choose the best course of treatment for the patient. But making those decisions while being surrounded by gunfire or hearing sirens was another matter altogether. Even when I was in Honduras, things didn't run as smoothly as here. It almost felt uncomfortable to be *this* comfortable.

When I entered the doctors' lounge, Dr. Robinson Matthew was there. He was the CEO of the hospital and someone I looked up to. He became the CEO last year, after a riding accident left him unable to perform surgeries.

"Maxwell, good to see you. How do you like it here?" he asked.

I bought a sandwich from one of the vending machines. It didn't look like much, but I was starving, and it would do. "The team is treating me great."

He barked out a laugh. He was in his sixties and an absolute legend. "You're something of a celebrity around here. We don't get many who've been abroad with Doctors Without Borders. The general usually steals them from us." *The general* was a nickname for the general hospital among the staff.

We sat down at one of the tables in the lounge. There were five in total, as well as a few couches. The cafeteria downstairs had more food to offer, but I didn't like that place as much. It was too crowded with staff, patients, and visitors. In between patients, I needed to be able to relax, and for that, I needed silence.

"You've accumulated a lot of knowledge and improved your technique, even while working under duress. You'll flourish here."

"Thanks. I think I will too."

"But you're still unwilling to sign a permanent contract?"

I swallowed the mouthful of sandwich I'd just bitten off before speaking, and it went down like dried sawdust.

"I don't want to make any rash decisions." I'd abandoned my work with Doctors Without Borders for Olivia. Since things didn't work out, there was theoretically nothing keeping me here except the possibility of opening a pro bono clinic. "I want to give hospital life a try before committing to it. It's a big change for me from what I used to do."

"Whenever you're ready to make it permanent, just say the word. We'll draft the contract before you have time to change your mind again."

"Interesting. I have thought about that—and you know what would make me sign right away."

He gave me a long look. "You drive a hard bargain, Maxwell."

"Always."

As CEO, Robinson Matthew could make the clinic happen. But he didn't question me any further on that. Instead he asked, "You're still living in your brother's hotel?"

"Yeah, but I'm going to look at a loft in half an hour. It's three streets away from the hospital, which is way more convenient."

Its proximity to the hospital was one of the reasons it caught my eye. The shifts were long and intense, and I didn't want to waste any time getting back home and crashing after a long day.

"Good luck with the apartment."

"Thank you."

I had a good feeling about it, and I had a good feeling about seeing Avery again too. Travis might give me shit, but I didn't care. She and I were grown-ups now, and I was looking forward to catching up with her.

After finishing my sandwich, I headed to the main floor to the locker room and changed quickly. I was out of the hospital in under five minutes.

The hospital and the loft were in the Pilsen neighborhood of the city, almost on the border of the South Loop neighborhood.

Before taking this job, I hadn't ventured here too often. I had to admit, the murals were famous for a reason. They looked like the art you'd find in a nice gallery.

It took a while for my eyes to adjust to the explosion of colors on the walls after staring at sterile white and gray the whole day, but I liked it. This area had a different vibe from where I'd grown up, and even different from the location I shared with buddies in college and med school. I checked my phone to make sure I was going in the right direction, and I arrived at the address a few minutes later. The building looked solid. It was a converted warehouse, and the ground floor had authentic redbrick walls. The upper level consisted of huge windows.

"Sam?"

I'd recognize her voice anywhere. Glancing to my right, I saw

Avery walking up to me. *Fuck me.* She looked exactly as I remembered but also different.

Her green eyes lit up. They'd always been one of the things I'd loved about her. Her blonde hair was long, covering her breasts. It was a few shades lighter than in high school.

"Hey, Avery. Great to see you again."

Her cheeks turned pink. I walked to her, leaning in and kissing her cheek. She smelled like flowers. Back in high school, she'd used a perfume with a minty note. I had no idea I'd memorized that detail about her.

I straightened up, taking a step back. I had this unbelievable feeling that I'd gone back in time.

"Are you ready to go up?" she asked. "We're supposed to be there in two minutes."

"Still a stickler for time, I see," I said, motioning for her to go in first.

"Do you still have a penchant for being late?"

"No. Being a doctor beat that out of me. Being late is not allowed. Ever."

"I can't believe you went through with it and became a doctor," she said as we entered the building. The door was wide open, which I didn't like. Did they leave it open on purpose for us, or was it an issue? It could become a security problem. I wasn't worried about myself, but if Avery did move in, I wanted her to be safe.

"Why not?" I asked. "I always said I would."

"I know, but we all dream about things when we're in high school." She looked over her shoulder. She was smiling, but it was tinged with resignation. "And then we change our dreams."

I had the sudden urge to bail on the open house and instead take her out for a drink and ask her about every detail of her life since the last time I saw her.

There was a sign in the inner courtyard with an arrow that said Open House. Good. That meant the door had been left open on purpose. We went up a staircase that looked old but was well maintained. It didn't smell moldy. It only went up six steps before the door of the apartment came into view. It was open, too, and I saw the realtor through it.

"This place is amazing," Avery marveled. "It has so much light."

"I agree," I said. It was four o'clock in the afternoon in October —not a bright month in Chicago, but being in here, you wouldn't know it.

The realtor came up to us. "Sam Maxwell and Avery Sinclair?"

"Yes," we said at the same time.

"Welcome. My name is Mal Dinklage, and I'll be showing you the property today."

"Are there others coming?" I asked.

"You've got a twenty-minute slot before the next appointment."

I narrowed my eyes at him. "You said I was the first one who contacted you."

"You were."

"Then I want the right to decide first."

He looked at me, stunned.

"Okay, that's… all right," Mal stumbled through his words. "Do you want me to show you around?"

I looked at Avery. "I think we can look on our own first and then come back with questions."

"Okay." He scurried to a window, looking outside. Avery was looking at me incredulously.

"What?" I asked.

"I don't know. The way you sounded earlier made it seem as if he didn't have a choice but to agree with you."

"And he didn't," I replied.

"Yeah, well, I'm still digesting how you went about it."

"Come on, let's look around," I said.

She walked in front of me. On instinct, I started to put my

hand at the small of her back but stopped myself at the last possible second.

What the hell? She's not your girlfriend, Sam. This is you and Avery sixteen years later. Fucking be a gentleman about it and behave.

"It's huge."

The main room was a vast space with an open floor plan that included a living room leading to the kitchen with a big island in the center. There was a full bath near the kitchen. It was at the foot of the staircase that led to the bedrooms upstairs. That was the only downside of the place—one bathroom only. There was a laundry room behind the kitchen, at least.

The bedrooms were very spacious. The furniture was included in the rental and consisted of a dresser, a huge bed, and a small desk in each room.

"This place is so huge," she said. "And so expensive. I mean, some people could afford it on their own, like you. Which reminds me…why do you need a roommate?"

"Look at this place. Like you said, it's far too big."

"Is this your only option?" she asked, playing with the pendant at the base of her neck.

It was a nervous tic. She'd always had it. I wondered how many other men knew this intimate detail about her.

Now I'm jealous of the guys she's been with in the last decade? I was toast. *What the hell is happening to me?*

"Yes. It's the only place with a flexible lease."

She turned to look at me from the doorway of the bedroom. "Why do you need a flexible one?"

"I'm not sure if I'm going to stay here for good."

"Oh."

Was it my imagination, or did she sound disappointed?

She licked her lips, running her hands through her thick, gorgeous hair, and then tugged at her right ear. It was another nervous tic. I had the overwhelming urge to close the distance and kiss her, find out if she'd react the same as all those years ago.

She used to make the most delicious sound just before she opened up for me, granting me access to her mouth.

Exhaling sharply, I turned, pretending to inspect the windowsill, trying to regain control.

"Why did you even come back?" she asked.

"That's a long story."

"Okay."

Looking up at her, I saw her twiddling her thumbs. "Avery, are you feeling uncomfortable?" I asked, getting straight to the point.

She shrugged, holding her hands up. "I don't know. This feels a bit weird."

I closed the distance again despite knowing it wasn't the best idea. The need to kiss her was back and even stronger than before.

"I don't know if moving in together is a good idea," she said. "I don't know you anymore. We're practically strangers."

"That's a risk you run with any roommate. Besides"—I tilted in closely until I could smell a whiff of her perfume again—"I wouldn't call us strangers."

"What would you call us?" she murmured.

I looked down at her lips before straightening up. I was teetering in dangerous territory. "I'm struggling to find the right words. 'Acquaintances' feels like a mouthful. And it doesn't even come close to describing us." I thought for a moment. "I have an idea. Why don't I take you out for a drink tonight? We'll spill our secrets. Then we won't be strangers anymore."

I looked her straight in the eyes, turning on my most charming smile. Her eyes rested on my mouth for a split second before she cleared her throat. I'd rattled her, which was exactly what I wanted.

"I can't. I promised I'd take Alana out."

"You're still friends with her?"

"I'm sleeping on her couch. She offered, even though we hadn't spoken basically since graduation."

"I see. So you have no problem camping out on her couch but hesitate moving in with me. I'm sensing the double standard."

She burst out laughing. "Touché."

"You will barely see me, Avery. I work all the time."

"How many hours per week is 'all the time'?"

"A hundred, give or take."

Her eyes bulged. "Give or take? That's like two jobs."

"I think it's going to be closer to eighty."

"Still two jobs."

"In that case, I'm going to be a great roommate."

She bit her lip, looking around. "I don't know. What if you do decide in a few months that you want to leave again, and then I'm left with all this rent?"

"I would never put you in a bad position, Avery. You know that."

"I see you still like to play knight in shining armor, huh? Then again, I guess that's why you became a doctor." She glanced around the loft. "Well, I have two more options that I'm going to look at this week."

Disappointment hit me like a fist. *What the hell?* I hadn't expected that.

When I'd first replied to her message in the alumni group on Facebook, it had been to extend a courtesy to the woman who once meant the world to me. I would've done anything for her back then, but then I lost her. When had it gone from that to *wanting* to share the apartment with her?

"I can take you and Alana out for drinks later," I offered. "I'd like to catch up with her as well."

"I don't think we can do that tonight, but it would be lovely to catch up at some point, even if this doesn't work out." She twirled her hair around her fingers, and I couldn't help but laugh.

"What?" she asked.

"You still have the same body language and mannerisms. It's a very odd sensation. I can't even describe it. It's like we're in the present but also in the past at the same time."

She smiled, pushing a strand of hair behind her ear. "I know what you mean. I had the exact same sensation when I saw Alana."

"Come on, let's go back downstairs. We don't want to run into the next visitors."

"Don't you want to check out the competition?" she asked playfully, looking at me over her shoulder.

"No."

"That's right. You intimidated that poor dude into practically giving you the apartment. I don't even think the others stand a chance."

"Good. They shouldn't."

"It's not yours just because you were the first one to contact him about it. You can't claim something simply because you were first."

Funny, because that was exactly what I wanted right now: to claim her.

Dammit, Sam, she used *to be yours. Not anymore.*

This evening was not going the way I wanted. I thought it would be a friendly catch-up. Instead, I was fighting every instinct not to kiss her.

As we walked through the living room, I instinctively reached out. This time I didn't catch myself and *did* put my hand on her back. She straightened sharply, looking at me sideways. I saw her swallow hard and dropped my hand. She flexed and then unflexed her fingers, playing with the ring on her middle one. I had a flashback to our first night together; she'd played with it just the same way before she told me she was ready.

"Thank you. The apartment is lovely. We'll let you know soon," she told Mal, who nodded.

We left just as two people came in. They looked like a couple and gave us the side-eye.

"Want me to drive you somewhere?" I asked her.

"No, thanks. I like strolling around the city a bit. I'll give you my answer this week."

"Okay. Say hi to Alana."

She was only a few steps away, and I felt her absence immediately. We had a connection after all these years, and that made me happy. Avery was the one who got away.

I was going to take the apartment anyway. The question was would she move in with me?

4

AVERY

*T*he next evening, I ran through the city at rush hour to see the only other apartment on my list. The second option I told Sam about went off the market this morning. I'd been working all day to rebuild my jewelry business from a coffee shop close to Alana's apartment, since she worked from home, and her place was too small for both of us to do that. I'd spent most of my time researching platforms that were easy for do-it-yourself websites. That was my starting point.

Up until three months ago, I'd been the proud co-owner of Jewels & Smiles, a cute and quaint shop in San Diego. I did all the designs and coordinated production, and Sophia, my so-called friend and business partner, took care of everything else on the business end. But then she misused our funds, so much so that we couldn't make payments. I hadn't been able to pay rent or the factory producing my designs, so I had no choice but to close down the business. Now I was back to square one. Actually, even worse. I was up to my eyeballs in debt. Sophia moved to New York after stealing all the company's money. I hadn't heard from her since.

A short, slim man with blond hair waited for me in front of

the apartment's door. Thomas Jenkins was the realtor.

"Thank you for coming on time," he said.

"Of course."

"It's a bit stuffy in here," he remarked as we stepped inside.

I cleared my throat. Stuffy was an understatement. Something stank inside here. I looked around, taking it in: carpeted floor, recently painted walls. The wooden frames of the doors were chipped in places, but it was normal wear and tear.

It was in a safe neighborhood. Not a trendy one, like the loft, but it would do.

After meeting Sam, I was convinced that Alana was right. I'd had the same déjà vu feeling with him as I'd had with her, only in his case, that included a severe case of wet panties and flutters in my stomach after sixteen years. Though it could've been a knee-jerk reaction to seeing him after all this time.

Sam hadn't changed much at all. The man was hot! I couldn't imagine living with him; I didn't think I could control myself. So this had to work out. It was a studio, which was perfect because I planned to buy a sofa bed similar to the one Alana had and call it a day. Still, the smell was persistent, and the longer I was inside, the more terrible it became.

Jenkins went to the window, opening it. The sound of the streets filtered in, and the noise was loud. It was Friday evening, and this was a lively neighborhood.

"This smell is getting worse the longer we stay here. Where is it coming from?" There was nothing rotten that I could see, though it wasn't even a scent of rot. It just seemed old.

He shook his head. "It's the damn carpet."

"Right," I said, my stomach sinking. The entire apartment was carpeted.

"It's been cleaned a couple times, but it's just damn old, and the owner refuses to change it."

If this was a permanent smell, no way would anyone live here. Could it really be the carpet?

I lowered myself to my haunches, and yep, he was right. I stood back up and walked around, thinking hard. I could bring my cleaning supplies, but from my experience, old, stinky carpets had to be replaced. They soaked up smoke and all other manner of odors over the years, and no matter how vigorously you scrubbed them, they still stank. I'd learned that when Mom, Jamie, and I moved into a dingy house, the first one we had in Chicago, and it smelled horrendously. We ended up changing the carpet at our own cost.

That gave me an idea.

"What if I buy a new one?" I suggested.

"That's a significant cost."

"I would lay it myself," I replied. "I know how to."

He shook his head. "The owner will never agree unless a professional does it."

I bit my lip, looking around. The place really would be great for me. Very small but welcoming. I could already imagine the setup. I'd have twinkle lights over the window. I could make it a home.

"Can you let me know by tonight?" he asked.

"Sure," I replied. After I left, I headed straight home. Alana had a work event in the evening and would be coming home later. I was going to surprise her by making dinner. My skills in the kitchen were limited, but I could make a very good quiche. It was all about the ingredients.

After setting everything I needed on the counter, I began cutting the leek and onions, then mixed them with a can of tuna along with a lot of cream before popping the dish in the oven. Dinner would be ready when she arrived home. I preferred using the oven for most of my cooking unless I was short on time, and then I'd use the microwave. Some people frowned upon using that for cooking, but it could be a trusty helper in the kitchen.

Alana came home just as I was pulling the dish from the oven.

"Honey, I'm home," she said, making me laugh. She kicked off her shoes by the entrance before joining me in the kitchen.

"Wow, you weren't kidding when you said you were making a quiche. I thought you were going to order it." She gave me a sheepish smile. "I've always wanted to come home to someone."

"That day will come," I said as I put huge slices on separate plates for us.

We sat down at the dinner table, and Alana ate it all quickly. I was glad she liked it.

"How was the apartment?" she asked.

"Honestly, not good," I said. "The carpet stinks."

Alana scrunched up her nose. "That's a huge no-no. You can't get that smell out of things no matter what you try."

"I know."

"So that was the only option, huh?"

"I saw another apartment on Craigslist on my way home. I'm going to check it out after dinner."

While we ate, she told me a bit about the event. Her job sounded glamorous, and it fit her perfectly. I was so happy that my friend had found her calling.

After we finished eating, I pulled out my laptop and looked at my other lead. "Oh, dammit. The listing says occupied already."

"Well, that's too bad. Do you have any others?"

"No."

"Look again. You never know. Maybe some new options popped up since you looked yesterday."

I doubted it. But then again, Chicago was a huge city. I opened three websites and put my filters in—studio and the maximum of rent I was willing to pay—and then pressed Search. Nothing came up.

I groaned. I could probably look for roommates on Craigslist, but did I really want to live with strangers?

"You're considering living with Sam," a small voice said at the back of my mind. But Sam wasn't a stranger in the real sense of the word. At one time, I knew him better than anyone else.

"What are you going to do?" Alana asked me. "Move in with Sam?"

"I don't know. I want to make a pro-and-con list."

She rose from her seat, opening the drawer of the sideboard behind her. "I can't believe you still do those. You need a paper and pen, right? Unless you do it digitally."

"No, still old-school paper and pen. It helps me decide when I see everything in front of me. Handwriting is a big part of it. Don't ask me why."

"Okay." She handed me a torn-off sheet of paper and a blue pen. "Sorry. I don't have colorful ones."

"Doesn't matter." In high school, I used to draw pros with pink, cons with blue.

I stared at the sheet of paper. In the pros list, I put the following: **great rent, amazing loft, close to work**.

I hesitated about the cons list before deciding on the biggest offenders.

1. Sam would be my roommate.

2. Sam is even hotter than he was in high school.

I took a deep breath before the third point, but I wrote it down because it was true.

3. I still react like a schoolgirl when I see him. It might be hard to resist him.

There it was, in black—or in this case, blue—and-white.

"So, what's the tally?" Alana asked. She sat across from me, putting her elbows on the table.

I held out the list for her.

She nodded. "Pretty much the way I imagined it. About that last point… Does he seem to have any sort of reaction to you?"

"I don't know," I admitted. "I was too busy trying to process the way I reacted to him to check for any signs that it was mutual."

"The way I see it, you don't have much to lose. You're going to live in a great place with a guy you might or might not have the hots for."

"Alana, you're not helping."

"What? I'm just stating the facts. If the attraction is one-sided, you have nothing to worry about. If it's mutual, you could jump his bones at some point." She said this so matter-of-factly, like she was talking about how we would split cleaning chores.

"You're a bad friend."

She gave me a wolfish smile. "I know, but I can't help myself. Don't you think maybe this is fate?"

I blinked rapidly. "What do you mean?"

"You've come back to Chicago, and suddenly you have an option to live with Sam."

"I also camped on your couch."

She rolled her eyes. "Yes, but you messaged me on Facebook, and we talked about it. But with Sam, it was, I don't know, serendipity, right? You replied to a post in the alumni group, and he happened to need an apartment at the same time." She shrugged. "Sounds like fate to me."

I pointed at Alana. "Stop. I don't like that road you're taking."

"If you say so."

"I do."

I swallowed hard. My chest felt a bit heavy. I remembered the times when I felt Sam and I were fated for each other, but that was a silly schoolgirl crush. Now I was a grown woman who'd lost her business and needed an affordable place to live while getting back on my feet.

"What are you going to do? Tell the hot doc that you're going to move in with him and possibly jump his bones?" She wiggled her eyebrows.

I rolled my eyes at her. "I'm going to look for some more apartments. You never know. Maybe something will come up. I still have a couple hours until I have to give him an answer." I sighed. "But yes, that's the gist of it."

5

SAM

"*A*re you trying to win the prize of being Paisley's favorite uncle?" Tate challenged my intentions.

"I'm definitely going to make a run for the title. I didn't even know it was up for grabs, but it's going to be mine before long." We were at his house in the Lincoln Park neighborhood, gathered for dinner. I'd forgotten how much my family loved cookouts. God, it was good to be back.

"I have a lot to make up to Paisley," I said as I helped my brother carry out the marinated chicken breast for the grill. Travis and Luke had already brought out the vegetables and other side dishes. We weren't fussy when it came to food, and the grilling season would end soon. October was the last decent month in Chicago as far as I was concerned.

"You've got a lot of competition," he said.

The truth was, because I'd been gone for so long, I hadn't been able to build a relationship with Paisley, not like the rest of my family had. I was a cool uncle because I always had stories from my travels. It was endearing the way her little eyes would light up whenever I recounted one. I tried to edit out any difficult information for her ears, so she'd only ever heard the good parts. But now that I was here, I wanted to do more, which was why I was negotiating with Tate to let me take my niece out for a treat, like ice cream.

"Buddy, you've missed that window."

"What window?" I asked as we went out in the backyard.

"When she thought going out for ice cream was a highlight. You're about two years too late."

"What does she like to do these days?"

"I think it's best if you ask her. It changes weekly."

My brother was about to have a teenager on his hands, and by the sound of it, he wasn't prepared in the least.

Outside, we set the meat on the grill. Declan was the man of the hour. He'd started putting on the potatoes first because they needed more time to cook. We were going to take turns at the grill because cooking for so many people was overwhelming.

I sometimes still couldn't believe that every single one of my brothers had a significant other. Over the past few years, I'd flown in for most of the events, like birthdays or big celebrations, such as when Travis sold his previous business— a successful software company. It felt like every time I came to visit, one more brother had gotten hitched.

"Until it's my turn on the grill, I'm going to check on Paisley," I said.

"Good luck," Tate replied before focusing on Declan. "Make sure the meat is overdone for Lexi, okay?"

"You only told me about fifty times," Declan replied.

I burst out laughing. "Okay, someone has to write this thing down in a calendar. The time when Tate was even more overbearing than Declan."

Lexi smiled, coming up to us. "Don't hate on him. He's a bit overprotective since I'm pregnant."

"Yes, obviously."

"You're a doctor. You should be on my side," Tate said.

"Cooking the meat is good. I'm hazing you for reminding Declan fifty times."

Lexi winked. "He's a little extra sensitive right now."

"Roger that." I winked before heading to Paisley. She was sitting in a patio chair with her iPad in her hand.

My parents and grandmother were sitting on a bench close to the grill. Tyler and his fiancée, Kendra, were chatting with Liz, Declan's fiancée. Luke and Megan stood a few feet away with our cousin Reese.

The only ones missing were Travis, Bonnie, and my niece, as well as our cousin Kimberly, who was in Paris—for now. Travis had convinced her to work with him to expand his hotel from a single unit to a chain. She was returning in a few months to help him with events and expansion.

"Hey, Paisley. How are you?" I asked.

She looked up at me. I could see the change in her from just half a year ago when she would light up and look at me like I was the most interesting person in the room. Now she was simply curious.

"Hey, Uncle Sam."

"So I've been talking to your dad, telling him that I want to take you out for ice cream, and he told me you like to do more interesting things these days."

She sat up straighter, pulling her knees to her chest. "Yes, I do. Ice cream is for kids."

Way to make me feel old. "Tell me, what would you like to do together?"

"Can I choose anything?" she asked.

"Sure. Why not?"

"I want to go shopping for makeup."

I blinked, jerking my head back. "That's not my area of expertise."

"You don't have to know anything. You just have to take me there, and the ladies at the counter will help."

"Is your dad okay with this?"

"He told you to take me out somewhere I want, didn't he?"

"This feels like a trap," I said out loud.

Paisley pressed her lips together.

"It *is* a trap," I added.

She didn't reply.

"You've inherited the Maxwell sneaky gene. I'm proud of you."

She gave me a cautious smile. "You are?"

"Obviously. It took us years to hone that, and you're a natural."

Her smile grew. "Then it means you'll take me to buy some makeup?"

"How about we don't give your dad a reason to skin me alive?"

She winced. "He wouldn't do that."

"No, that's a figure of speech, Paisley." A damn graphic one. Why had I even used it? I wasn't used to being around kids, but I was going to learn and do better from now on.

"Dad says you're staying for longer this time."

"Yeah."

"So you're not going to leave again?"

"I'm not sure," I admitted.

"We all miss you, you know, and Gran and Great-Gran most of all. Actually, I think everyone misses you, but they're the only ones who say it out loud. The rest feel like their balls will drop off or something if they admit it."

My eyes widened. "Excuse me?"

She cringed. "Whoops. Don't tell anyone I said that. They still don't know how much I can swear."

"How can you even swear like that?" I spluttered.

"I picked it up."

"From where?"

"Everywhere: school, everyone's conversations when you think I'm not listening."

"Exactly how much are you eavesdropping?" I asked.

"A lot, especially because everyone seems to think I'm still too small to pick up on things. But I know stuff. Girls at my school have boyfriends already."

I looked over my shoulder. "Does your dad know that?"

"No, because he's my dad," she said as if this was the most obnoxious question she'd ever heard. "And no one else does either, but I figured you're the youngest brother. And the coolest."

"Yes," I said tentatively, suspicious of where this conversation was going.

"So, that means you're closest to my age."

By about two decades. I nodded her on.

"You can give me advice."

"On what?"

She rolled her eyes. "Boys."

I was so out of my depth, I didn't have a name for it.

"What are you two chatting about?" Gran asked, walking up to us. She had a familiar look in her eyes, and I knew she had my back. She could read me like an open book.

"Boys," Paisley said nonchalantly.

Gran didn't seem surprised in the least. "I see. My advice wasn't helpful?" she asked politely.

I felt like I'd stepped into a science-fiction movie.

"It was, but I think I also need a male perspective on this, and everyone else is so old."

I looked over my shoulder at my brothers huddled around the grill. I had to find a way to warn Tate while also not breaking Paisley's confidence. My brother had to know what was coming for him; otherwise, he'd be completely blindsided.

I soon found my angle. I was going to talk to Lexi first.

"I'm going to help everyone over by the grill. Gran, Paisley, you need anything?"

"No, no, we're both fine," Gran said. "It's good having you back home, Sam."

Heading back to the grill, I eyed Lexi. I needed to work my way into this.

"Can I talk to you for a second?" I asked.

She looked at me in surprise. "Sure." She was holding two pieces of chicken on her plate. I looked at it intently.

"Okay, that one needs to go back on the grill. It's still too pink."

Lexi smiled. "Yes, I saw that. That's why I wasn't eating it. And you were making fun of Tate. Pot and kettle, aren't you?"

"I'm a doctor," I replied. "And a man as well. I guess overprotectiveness comes with the territory. And speaking of overprotectiveness…" I glanced at Paisley and then back at Lexi.

"What's wrong? Did something happen to her?"

"No, the overprotectiveness is toward my big brother."

"What are you talking about?"

"I have a feeling he's going to be blindsided."

Lexi lowered her plate, looking at me intently. "Sam, you're scaring me."

"Paisley's talking about boys."

"Oh yeah, I know," she said as nonchalantly as Gran.

"And this is fine?" I asked, dumbfounded.

"Why wouldn't it be?"

"She's eleven."

"She just turned twelve."

I rolled my eyes. "I'm sorry. Yes, twelve."

"Of course she's curious. I'm surprised she told you."

"She said she wants the male perspective." I looked over my shoulder. Fortunately Tate wasn't in earshot.

He was going to find out about it sooner rather than later, but I was determined not to be the one who conveyed the news.

Lexi chuckled. "She did tell me she wants a well-rounded perspective. Don't worry about this. I'm handling it, okay?"

I trusted Lexi with a lot of things, but I wasn't sure about this at all.

"Okay, everyone, the meat is ready. Grab something before it's all gone," Declan announced.

There was a frenzy of activity around the grill as everyone approached it with plates, choosing their food.

I grabbed pork chops and grilled zucchini, and then we all sat down at the huge table my brother had set up in the middle of his yard. It hadn't been here last time I visited, but we'd outgrown the outdoor furniture he'd had before. There were simply too many of us. This was a folding table, so we would move it out of the way when we were done.

While we were eating, my phone pinged. As a general rule, I never ignored my phone, even if I wasn't on call, just in case the hospital might need me. The message was from Avery, though. It was short and to the point.

Avery: Hey, Sam, if you're still looking for a roommate, I'm in.

I heard the angels singing, and my chest exploded.

Fuuuuuuuuuck yeeeeeeeeees. I felt triumphant.

"What's with that Cheshire-cat smile?" Mom asked.

"You probably all remember Avery. We dated in high school. Anyway, to cut the story short, we're both interested in the same loft. We're going to be roommates for a while."

The next few moments were downright comical. First, everyone sitting next to me stopped talking: Tate, Lexi, Liz, and Declan. Then the others fell silent, too, probably wondering why no one was saying a word.

"What's happening?" Luke asked. He was at the other end of the table.

"You dated? You're moving in with your ex-girlfriend?" Paisley exclaimed.

"Paisley, she's a friend now," I said patiently. "It's not what you're all thinking. This is platonic."

She scoffed. "My friends at school say there's no way you can be friends with an ex-boyfriend. It's forbidden."

"Your friends at school have ex-boyfriends?" Tate burst out.

I exchanged a glance with Lexi, who cringed. That train hit

my brother without any warning, as I feared. I just didn't think it would happen so fast.

"We're drifting off the point," Paisley said. "The focus was on Uncle Sam." She was surprisingly efficient as a moderator.

Tate wasn't saying anything else, but that could just be because he was too dazed. Everyone else turned to look at me.

"Son, are you sure that's a good idea?" Mom asked me. "You and Avery were very close. First loves don't just fade away."

I looked around the table. "Can we please continue what we were doing before? This is very awkward. I simply wanted everyone to know I'd be moving out of the hotel. It's not up for debate."

Tyler patted my shoulder. "Dude, I think you forgot how things happen in this family. Everybody discusses everything to death and offers you their opinion."

"Everyone has already offered their opinion," I said.

"No, we haven't," Luke chimed in.

I looked straight at Declan, who, to my astonishment, said nothing. I didn't seem to be the only one weirded out by this. He was always the quickest to point out what could go wrong.

"What, no warning to give him?" Luke asked.

"I can't see any legal repercussions from this. Still not sure if it's a good idea."

"I don't need anyone to vote on it," I grumbled.

"Why do you even need a roommate?" Luke asked.

"I don't. We both showed our interest in the space simultaneously, and *she* needs a roommate. I like the loft—"

The look in his eyes was triumphant, and it derailed my train of thought. I didn't like it, but I didn't question it, because I honestly didn't want to know.

"Hmm. Well, I tend to agree with your mom," Kendra said. "It might not be the best of ideas."

"Unless…," Megan said.

"Unless what?" I asked.

"You're planning to... you know. Get back with her." She wiggled her eyebrows. I liked her a lot. She was very feisty.

"Damn, I didn't think about that," Tyler said. "Are you?"

I burst out laughing. "God, I forgot what it was like with you all."

"Yeah, we should ease the guy in," Reese said. "We don't want to scare Sam off. He isn't even in the WhatsApp group. Now we're suddenly overwhelming him with... I'm not even sure if I should call this advice."

"No, it's called *opinionating*," Paisley said confidently.

I smiled again. I was happy to be back, even though I'd lost my touch. I had no idea how to handle this conversation. Especially since the last time everyone butted into my life, my brothers had been single. Now I had twice as many opinions.

"This is good, Uncle Sam," Paisley said, "because you'll get a female perspective on it."

"I wasn't even aware I needed a female perspective," I said. "Or any sort of perspective. But by all means, pitch in."

"Oh, we weren't going to stop," Tate said.

"Or ask for permission," Reese added.

"We were just taking a moment to process everything," Luke finished.

Duly noted. The Maxwell clan had sharpened their skills over the years, and I was playing catch-up. But not for long.

"Anyone care to share the story with me?" Lexi asked. "I don't believe I know it in full."

"And we can't offer our advice without knowing it," Megan agreed. "How long were you together? Was it serious?"

Gran looked at me before glancing at Paisley. Considering she knew the expression "balls dropping off," I couldn't see how my story would be worse for her ears.

"Avery and I dated for two years in high school."

"They were prom king and queen," Mom said. "And I honestly

thought they'd marry right after college. But then they broke it off as soon as prom was over."

"Mom, would you like to tell the story?" I asked.

She ignored me and said, "But I don't know the whole story."

I swallowed hard, putting my fork down. I hadn't thought about that evening for years. Did I want to drag it all up?

"Her mom got sick, and she had to move out of the city to take care of her. Just before she left, she said it wouldn't make sense to keep dating while we were apart." In the blink of an eye, things just ended. I'd wanted to be there for her, help her with her mom. But she categorically refused.

My chest constricted. Even after all these years, losing her felt like a punch to the gut.

"Okay, see that expression on his face? It tells me your mom is on to something," Lexi said in a fake whisper.

"Yeah, dude. Are you still mooning over her?" Tyler asked.

I stared at him. "I already agreed to this, and I'm not going to go back on my word, even if you're disagreeing with me."

"Oh, we're not disagreeing," Luke said. "We're just going to enjoy watching you fall. Last Maxwell brother standing." He winked. "But not for long."

6

SAM

"Remind me why no one in this family believes in hiring movers," Travis said one week later. I was moving into the loft, and I'd enlisted the help of all my brothers.

"I think our family policy is great," Declan said seriously. Dad had drilled into us at a young age that you don't pay anyone else to do something you can do yourself. We all lived by it, even Travis, although he did so grudgingly.

"Why pay a moving company when I can ask you all to do it for free?" I teased as Luke and I carried the couch inside.

"I agree," Tyler said. He was carrying a huge box.

"Maybe because we all have much better things to do. I have a wife and a newborn," Travis grumbled.

He and Tate were each carrying trash bags containing clothes and other odds and ends over their shoulders. I didn't have many things to begin with, since I'd been gone for so many years. The couch had been in storage. I'd had it in the first apartment I shared with friends in college.

"The couch smells old. I think I might change it soon," I said after positioning it by the wall.

Declan stared at me. "Dude, I think we should add an addendum to the family policy. Don't make anyone work just for fun."

"It's not for fun," I said. "I knew I had a couch, and I didn't bother looking for another one." The loft had furniture except for a couch. I'd asked Avery what she thought about it, and she'd liked it.

"The place looks good," Luke said appreciatively, glancing around. "Modern."

"I like the neighborhood too," Tyler added.

"Yeah. It just has one problem," Travis said.

I snapped my head at him. "What?"

It seemed good enough to me, but I wasn't an expert on buildings. Neither was Travis, though.

He grinned. He was about to give me shit.

"I don't think it's big enough to cut through the sexual tension between you and Avery."

"Man, what are you talking about? There's nothing going on," I said.

"For now," Luke said with a wink.

Tyler chuckled. "I'm with Luke on this one."

My brothers were unbelievable. Declan was the only one who didn't seem intent on making fun of me.

I carried the trash bags into my room. I was going to deal with them later. Everything I owned in terms of clothing was in them; it would take no time at all to put them in the dresser.

Going back to the living room, I planned to ask my brothers if they wanted to stay for dinner. There were a bazillion hip restaurants around. We could order something in, or I could take them out for a drink. But when I came in, Tate was on the phone with Paisley. Travis was also on the phone, probably with Bonnie. Maybe Travis wasn't just teasing me; my brothers had their own lives to go back to.

A bout of guilt hit me that I'd made them all come here. Dad's rule was reasonable, but my intention hadn't been to take my brothers away from their families.

"Guys, thanks for your help. I think we're all done here."

Declan cocked a brow. "You sure?"

"Yes."

"When is your girl moving in?" Tate asked. He'd finished his conversation and was pocketing his phone.

"She's not my girl, she's my roommate, and she should've been here ten minutes ago, at seven o'clock."

"See? We need to give you shit now so we get it out of our system before she arrives."

As if on cue, the doorbell rang, and Travis winked at me. "We can't very well let her carry her stuff in on her own, can we?"

"She wouldn't be on her own," I remarked. "I'd help her."

"Yeah, but the more the merrier, that's what I say."

"Unless, of course, we're interrupting something. Are we?" Tyler asked.

"I forgot you're such a buffoon."

"I'm always glad to remind you," he replied with a wide grin.

We all headed downstairs. Avery was by the entrance with a huge suitcase and five boxes.

I reached her first. "Where's the rest of your stuff?" I asked.

"This is everything I have."

"My brothers will be disappointed."

Her eyes widened. "They're here?"

"Yes." I had a hard time keeping my eyes on her face. She was wearing short cutoff jeans, and her legs seemed endless. Her skin looked so soft that I barely bit back the impulse to move closer and find an excuse to touch her. I remembered the way her skin felt under my fingers. It was all Travis's fault that I was fantasizing.

The next second, my brothers came down.

"Hey, all the Maxwells are here," Avery said with a laugh. "Let me guess, honoring the family policy. 'Don't hire someone to do stuff for you,' right?" She frowned, running a hand through her hair, and bit her lower lip. My cock twitched. I was on a dangerous slope already.

"No, it's 'Don't pay anyone to do stuff you can do yourself,'" Luke explained. He nodded at her boxes. "That's all you have?"

"Yep. That's all I own: my suitcase and these five boxes."

"Do you still have stuff in storage?" Tate asked.

Her eyes dimmed. "No."

"Then this will be quick," Tyler said.

I trained my gaze on her. She looked vulnerable, hurt, and I needed to know why.

"Come on. Don't stand around, make yourselves useful. Each of you grab a box. I'll take this suitcase," I instructed, and everyone followed.

Avery whistled appreciatively. "Wow. Has the chain of command changed in the family? I don't remember Sam ordering you all around when we were kids."

Declan winked at her. "He doesn't. We're just playing nice because you're here."

"Okay. Duly noted," Avery said as we went up the staircase. "It's so surreal to see you all again."

She was walking in front of us all, and I was the first one behind her. Keeping my eyes away from her ass was becoming more difficult with every step. It looked perfect from this angle. Avery had filled out, and I loved it—lots of curves with a slender waist. Yeah, she was perfect.

She looked over her shoulder. "Any of you married now? Wait, I think I read that Tyler is engaged, right? And Travis too. There's been stuff in the media."

That last statement earned a collective groan.

She gasped, looking over her shoulder. "What?"

As we stepped inside, I said, "We're not on friendly terms with the media."

Avery sighed. "I remember you were never fans. They were

45

vicious when you were younger. It's like they kept expecting you all to mess up because your family was well-off. But you didn't."

Had she kept tabs on my family? Then again, it wasn't hard. The press didn't write about us often, mostly because we didn't give them any fodder. But when they could sink their teeth into something, they made a spectacle out of it. And the name Maxwell was still a magnet for gossip.

Avery put her fingers on her lips as if zipping them up. "Sorry I brought this up. Consider it forgotten."

"Where do you want the boxes?" Tate asked.

"Just take them up to my room. Thanks, guys."

I went up with the suitcase first. It was heavy as hell. *What did she pack in it?* It didn't matter; it was none of my business. I put it next to the dresser, and my brothers stacked the boxes on the desk opposite the bed.

"Man, she's still smoking hot," Travis said. "And I'm saying that in a completely objective way because, as we all know, I'm a very happily married man."

"Yes, we know that, Travis. You rub it into our faces every chance you get," Declan said.

Travis shrugged. "It's not my fault you're dragging your feet about setting a wedding date."

"No one's dragging anything," Declan said. "Liz is busy establishing the bakery, and I respect that."

That was a mark of how much he cared about Liz. Declan was impatient, and he certainly liked things done his way.

Tyler cleared his throat. "We're all doing things at our own pace."

Tate was looking at me suspiciously.

"What?" I asked.

"I saw the way you looked at her."

Tyler chuckled. "I wasn't going to say anything, but since Tate brought it up, I agree with him."

"I didn't ask anyone," I reminded them.

"Fair enough," Luke said.

"That means we'll abstain from giving our opinions," Declan said. He was surprising me more and more.

We all headed back downstairs and into the kitchen. I stopped midway because my phone beeped with a message. It was from Paisley.

Paisley: Uncle Sam, would you say being a nerd is COOL?

I pondered this. She randomly sent me texts from time to time, and I always made a point to give her a smart answer, not just a brush-off.

Sam: Being yourself is cool. Don't try to pretend for others.

Paisley: Are you sure? What if people stop liking me?

Sam: Then they aren't true friends.

Paisley: Thank you, Uncle Sam.

I was slowly realizing that I wouldn't be her favorite uncle any time soon—my brothers had spoiled her for far too many years, and I couldn't match that—but I liked being her confidante. I shoved the phone back in my pocket and joined the group in the kitchen.

Avery was gulping down a glass of water. Damn, she was sexy. Her chest was rising and falling in quick beats. Her throat was pulsing with the effort of swallowing the large amount of water quickly.

She smiled sheepishly at all of us. "I'm sorry. I was just so damn thirsty the whole way over here. Do you guys want something to drink?"

"No, we're good," Tate replied.

"We're just curious about you," Travis said.

Avery smiled playfully. "Still straight to the point. I remember that about you."

Since Travis was closest to my age, she'd dealt with him more than the rest of my brothers. "How come you came back to Chicago?" Travis asked, and I practically saw Avery shrink in front of my eyes. She didn't want to talk about it, which meant it was still a raw wound.

I wanted to get to the bottom of it and find out what she'd been through the past sixteen years, but I was definitely not going to let my brother corner her into talking. Not that that was his intention. He probably thought he was just making conversation.

"Travis, weren't you just telling me earlier how much of an asshole I am for taking you away from your wife and daughter? Why don't you all call it a night, and we can catch up another time after Avery and I have time to settle in?" I suggested.

"You have a daughter?" Avery asked, eyes wide and warm.

Travis nodded, smiling widely. "Yeah. Newborn. Barely two weeks old."

"Oh, that's lovely. What's her name?"

"Rose."

"I love it. Congratulations."

"Thank you." He was still looking at Avery, but he'd noticed the change in her expression. He didn't push. Instead, he looked around the group. "Okay, gang, let's go and let these two get settled in."

"Call us if you need anything," Declan said.

Luke glanced around. "Yeah. Any issue you have, let me know. I can help. I can find professionals to deal with everything."

"Thanks, man," I said. "I really appreciate that." I had a high tolerance toward broken stuff—I'd lived in all sorts of accommodations while abroad—but I wanted Avery to have all the comforts possible.

As soon as my brothers left, she poured herself another glass of water, drinking it up. It was impossible to ignore how damn sexy she was. Her body was like a dream. She had curves in all the right places, and I remembered exactly how they felt in my hands.

7

SAM

I walked up to her on the other side of the kitchen island. When she downed the last glass, she sighed loudly.

"That's good. I feel like I'm reborn. I was running around like crazy today."

"You could've told me. I would've sent one of the Maxwell bozos to help you."

She laughed. "Oh no, that's fine. Trust me. It was just crazy busy. But good busy, you know?"

I wanted to ask her what bad busy was, but I refrained.

"So, what do your brothers do? I know Tyler plays hockey, but what about the rest?"

"Each of us went on a different path. Tate owns a wine business, Declan is a lawyer, Luke has an architecture company, and Travis sold his software company a couple years ago and has now opened a hotel. It's in the same building as The Happy Place."

"Your grandmother kept the bookstore?"

"Yes. She still goes there a few times a week."

The Happy Place was the first store Gran and Grandfather ever opened, and she'd wanted to keep it.

"Beatrice always was a spitfire."

"Travis opened his hotel above it, so he's keeping an eye on Gran too."

"Oh, that's right. I read that in the news." She frowned. "Did I upset him earlier by mentioning the press?"

"No. We're all holding a grudge since they called Bonnie, his wife, a gold digger."

Avery gasped.

"And a few years ago, they targeted Reese," I continued. "She had to cancel her wedding at the last minute, and the press was all over it."

"That sounds terrible. Poor Reese. As if canceling your wedding isn't bad enough." Glancing around, she added, "Should we set some house rules?"

I detected a tinge of nervousness in her voice.

"Rules?" I asked blankly.

"Yes. You know, boundaries or guidelines." She moved her shoulders playfully, and it reminded me of her dance moves at prom.

"How do you usually do things with your roommates?" she asked.

"I bunked up with doctors mostly. We barely saw one another, and no one had a private life. There was no need for guidelines. How about you?"

"All right, so…"

Am I making her nervous? I rounded the kitchen counter, coming closer to her.

"Avery?"

"Yes?" she asked, jumping a bit.

"You don't have to be nervous. It's me."

She pushed a strand of hair behind her ear. "How do you know I'm nervous?"

"Instinct," I replied. " You still have the same cues you had back when we were together."

"Aha!" She pointed at me. "So… some things should be off-limits."

"What?" I asked, confused.

"We shouldn't talk about the fact that we dated in high school."

"Why not?"

"I just think it's easier, you know?"

I didn't, but if it made her comfortable, I was willing to go with it.

"Okay. Next topic. I printed my schedule for the week." I pointed to the fridge. "Do you mind if I keep it here? I like to have it at a glance."

Her eyes widened as she looked at it. "You're gone a lot."

That made me laugh. "I told you that you wouldn't see much of me."

"Right, but… a lot, a lot. Do you ever sleep?"

"Yeah," I said.

"It doesn't look like it."

"The shifts can change, but I still like to print it out and have it here. It's better than always looking at the calendar on my phone."

"I see you always start at the crack of dawn. That means I'll have no competition for the bathroom in the morning." She smiled nervously. "We do need guidelines for that, right? So we don't accidentally…"

"Walk in on the other one naked?" I finished for her.

She gasped. "Sam, do you enjoy putting me on the spot?"

"I fucking do," I replied on instinct.

I tilted a bit closer. She bit her lip. *Fuck me.* Travis was 100 percent right about the sexual tension.

She narrowed her eyes. "All right. We also need a code of conduct for when the other person has a guest."

"What do you mean, a code? We just have to be civil."

"No, I mean a sexy guest. Should we use the college code of a sock on the door or something?"

I felt like she'd smacked me right in the face. For the first time, the implication of living with her fully hit me. What if she brought a dude home and took him into her room? I'd go insane.

Absolutely not. I wanted to make it a code of conduct that she wasn't allowed to bring a man home ever. Not even once.

Logically, I knew I was being absurd. What did that even say about me?

She smirked. "Oh, you like to give but not get, huh? You forget, I have just as much sass as you. That hasn't changed from high school."

"Good to know. I always loved that about you."

She pointed at me, but I shook my head. "You brought it up first."

"I didn't." Closing her eyes, she shrugged. "Fine. I hinted at it. My bad. Won't happen again."

"This is going to be fun," I said.

"Oh yeah?" she murmured.

We'd only officially moved in together a few minutes ago, and we were already verbally sparring. I liked where this was going.

"Okay, so since we settled that, how about I take you out to dinner?" I asked her.

"I'd take you up on it, but I'd have to change, and I have no energy for that. How about we order something in and christen this place?" she asked and then covered her mouth. I started to laugh and couldn't stop. "I did not mean that as a double entendre."

I put a hand on the kitchen counter, close to her waist. "You didn't? Are you sure? Not even a little bit?"

She groaned, lowering her head. "I'm not sure what's happening to my brain right now."

"I don't know either, but I like it," I admitted. I was close enough again to smell her perfume. For my own sanity, I took a huge step back.

She pulled out her phone, licking her lips. Her fingers trembled slightly as she brought up a food ordering app.

"What are we in the mood for?" she asked.

"Pizza?"

"Yeah, let's do that."

I didn't care. I was more eager about the christening part.

"I have drinks," I said.

She snapped her head up. "You went shopping?"

"Nah. Courtesy of Tate."

"Oh, that's right. I forgot. Maxwell Wines. I love them so much."

"Which one's your favorite?" I asked, heading to the box my brother had deposited on the kitchen counter.

"The chardonnay."

"I've got one of those."

"Perfect. I take it as a good omen," she said as I rose to my feet, putting the bottle on the counter.

"For what?" I asked.

She hesitated before answering. "Starting over." She took two glasses from the cabinet as I opened the bottle. While I poured our wine, she ordered pizza. Then we clinked glasses.

"To new beginnings, then," I said. "What exactly are you trying to put behind you?" I asked after she took her first sip.

She closed her eyes, opening them again after a few beats. "I thought this might come up."

"We don't have to talk about it. I just wondered."

"Oh, I think we do," she replied. "Otherwise, it kind of feels like there's this big thing, you know? That makes things awkward now and again."

"Like when Travis put you on the spot?"

She shook her head. "I just wasn't expecting it, that was all." She looked at me speculatively.

"I'd love to know what you've been up. Want me to go first?" I offered.

"You've read my mind. Why are you back in Chicago?" she asked.

"Initially, I wanted to come back because I was in a long-distance relationship. Thought moving back would be the only way to give it a real try."

She grimaced. "And judging by the fact that you are now living with a roommate, it didn't work out."

"Turns out she still wanted to play the field. I found out the hard way. She was in bed with another guy."

She covered her mouth with her hand. "Sam, that's awful. I'm so sorry."

"It is what it is," I said, shrugging and taking another sip. "So, that's my story."

She played with the stem of her glass.

"Mine's about betrayal too," she mumbled. "Except it wasn't a romantic thing. My friend and business partner cheated me out of my own business."

"What?" I asked. "Wait, what is your business?"

"I'm a jewelry designer, even though I have no designs left to my name and no shop."

She rolled her shoulders, holding her chin high.

"You always said you wanted your own jewelry shop."

"Yes, I did."

I remembered that conversation after prom, when she said her mom got sick, so they had to move out of Chicago, relocate somewhere less expensive. She told me dreaming wasn't for people like her, that she had to put her head down and get to work, focus on getting through the day.

"I went to community college while I took care of Mom, and once she was back on her feet, I transferred to a jewlery design program."

"Smart. How is your mom?"

"Great. She's retired in Florida."

I nodded. "She always talked about moving back there. And

Jamie?"

"Lives in Maine. She's an accountant. I should've taken her up on her offer of doing my accounting." She kept playing with the stem of her glass. "About five years ago, I finally started my jewelry business. I had an online shop, but it wasn't really working out, so I opened a small location with a moderate amount of inventory. It was great. For a while. Anyway, I met this woman, Sophia," she continued. "She was saying all the right things, even giving me ideas for expansion. She wanted to be my partner, and I didn't give it another thought. I was excited to build something together with her. She'd had successful companies of her own, and it just made sense. Fast-forward two years, and I found out she was using the company as her own personal ATM. There's nothing left," she murmured.

"Fuck it. Let's go after her. Let's sue her," I said.

She smiled, but it was sad. "Oh, Sam, you're a doctor."

"Declan is a lawyer. He's a damn good one, and he's making it his priority to protect the family."

"I'm not family. I'm just a fool who didn't even think about hiring a second lawyer to look over the contracts. Sophia was in cahoots with our lawyer. She was very thorough and apparently had it all planned so I couldn't go after her. Believe me, I tried. There's a clause saying we can't sue each other."

"Avery—" I started, but she shook her head.

"Let's not get into it. I just wanted to put it out in the open so you don't think I'm a fugitive from the law or something."

"I didn't think that," I replied.

She smiled playfully. "Are you implying that you don't think I can be up to no good?"

"Oh, I know you can be."

She closed her eyes. "Okay. Before…my brain had a slip, but now I'm blaming the wine."

"I wonder what you're going to blame next time," I said with a wiggle of my eyebrows.

"There will be no next time. Anyway, now it's me and an online store, and I'm very excited about it. I was going to create a website myself, but I think I'll just end up using Etsy. It's easier to draw traffic there."

I furrowed my brow. "I don't understand. What happened to the physical store?"

"There was no cash left in the company for paying the lease, or the inventory, or anything."

Fuck me. I was going to ask Declan to look into this Sophia person. She couldn't just get away with it.

Avery shook her head. "Please, let's not talk about it. This evening was off to such a great start."

"Despite all the innuendos and slips?" I added, making her laugh.

Her cheeks went pink. "Yes, despite that." She chuckled. "I think it was foolish to think there would be none of that."

The bell rang, making us both jump.

"The pizza was fast," she said.

I went to the door, opening it and paying the delivery boy.

When I headed back to the kitchen, Avery was taking the plates from a drawer. I thought her ass looked perfect before on the stairs, but it was nothing compared to now. She was bending at the waist, her ass up in the air, and I had no idea how I managed to stifle a groan. She straightened up with two plates, completely red in the face. Her hair was wild around her head as she turned to look at me, and my mind immediately went to a dirty place.

I imagined her looking exactly like that while she moved up and down on my cock.

Sam, don't be an asshole.

We'd just moved in, and I was already having trouble controlling myself. She'd opened up to me. She was in a vulnerable place, and I wasn't going to take advantage. I was going to be the perfect roommate, an exemplary gentleman... for now.

8

AVERY

The first week of living with Sam went by in a breeze. The man was almost never at home. I'd successfully managed to avoid seeing him naked when he came out of the shower.

Though I did take a delicious peek when he'd gone to the kitchen one evening late at night. He'd only had a towel wrapped around his waist as he made himself a sandwich, and I'd spied on those gorgeous abs of his. Only from a distance, of course. I'd stopped on the staircase when I noticed he was in the living room. But even from a distance, it was obvious his body was very toned. The lines of his abs and arms were extremely well defined.

During the day, I had the loft all to myself. I spent the entire week building up my Etsy store. It was a completely different beast from owning my own website, but anything I built would look amateur, and I didn't have money to hire a pro to do it.

I hoped that directing my current clients to the shop was going to kick-start the algorithms. One could only hope. I was very positive about it.

I'd also emailed half a dozen factories. I needed someone to produce my designs, after all. Not that I was working on designing much these days. I'd made an account on Fiverr, a website dedicated to pairing freelancers with customers, offering my design services. I'd done a few courses of general graphic design, so I was hoping to make some money with that too.

At seven o'clock, I closed my laptop. I'd had enough for one day. My eyes were dry and burning. I rapidly blinked a few times until they felt better.

I headed to the kitchen, inspecting Sam's schedule on the fridge. *Wait, he wasn't on call last evening?* As far as I could tell, he hadn't been home. But according to the sheet, he'd been free yesterday and was on call today.

I took out a prewashed packaged salad and tossed it into a bowl. It was my trick for eating more veggies. I put in sun-dried tomatoes and artichokes dipped in olive oil, then dumped precooked garbanzo beans in it. I was just drizzling balsamic vinegar over it when the front door opened, and Sam came in.

"Hey, you're home," I said.

He looked utterly exhausted. He had dark circles under his eyes, and his shoulders seemed to have a heavy weight pressing on them. "Last evening was a clusterfuck, and I had to stay, so they gave me tonight off instead."

He groaned, dipping his head back. I had the greatest urge to reach out and give him a neck or shoulder rub or something. Oh dear Lord, my brain was coming up with the most inventive excuses to touch him. But I was determined to be on my best behavior. Living with Sam was easy when he wasn't at home. But every time we were in the same room, my entire body simmered.

"I made a salad. We can share it. It's huge."

He looked at it suspiciously. "Beans and green leaves?"

"Yeah, I know. It's super healthy, right?"

"Why did you make so much?"

"I thought about keeping some for tomorrow at lunch, but as I said, I'm happy to share."

He nodded. "I'll take you up on that. Thanks." He drummed his fingers on the kitchen counter. They were so long and sexy.

Brain, stop. Fingers aren't sexy. It's simply not a thing.

"Do you mind waiting a bit? I want to take a shower to freshen up."

"Sure. I'm not starving and don't mind waiting at all," I said. "I was going to make some toast as well, if you want some."

"Thanks. I'd really appreciate that. Good to see you." He leaned in, kissing my cheek.

I sucked in a breath because it had been totally unexpected. Feeling his lips on my cheek sent my senses into overdrive. I held my breath as he straightened up, winking at me.

"Damn, I forgot to take the laundry out of the dryer," he said as he went into the bathroom at the bottom of the staircase.

I took out a pan and was determined to keep my eyes on it. The washing machine and dryer were in a small room behind the kitchen, so after he was done showering, he'd pass right in front of me.

That's okay, Avery. Stay cool as a cucumber.

I put a bit of butter on the toast—in my humble opinion, butter made everything a million times better. Then I set the table. I moved my notebook to the edge of it, since I'd taken up the dining room table as my office. Even though I had a desk in the bedroom, there was simply more space and light here.

When I heard the bathroom door open, I stilled, peeking from the corner of my eye. *Oh hell no.* He was only wearing a towel. My little heart couldn't handle this. I moved very precisely with the intention of trying not to look at him, which, of course, made me bump into the corner of the table.

"Ow," I cried, stumbling backward into the kitchen island.

Sam came up to me right away. "Are you okay?"

"Yeah, yeah. I just wasn't paying attention and bumped into the table."

"Where did you hit?"

"My thigh."

He was so close that my mind became a blur. I didn't think I'd be in such proximity with his abs so quickly. I hadn't braced myself for this.

"I was distracted," I mumbled.

"By what?" His eyes were more alert. He seemed so much more awake than before. That shower had a magical effect on him.

I cocked a brow. "Can you put on some clothes?"

"Oh, I see. You see me half naked and bump into table corners."

"Sam," I admonished. "You find this funny?"

He threw his head back, laughing. His Adam's apple bobbed up and down. "I find it hilarious."

Seeing him laugh made me laugh too. I took a step back for a good measure, and he was the first one who seemed to regain his breath.

"Okay. I'll take mercy on you and no longer distract you. I'll go to my room and change."

"Yes, please do." I put the back of my hand theatrically to my head. "How else can I resist your holy hotness?"

His eyes glinted, and I swallowed hard, realizing what I'd implied. I cast my gaze to the table again and focused on splitting the salad as evenly as possible between our two plates.

Thankfully, he went to the laundry room for his clothes and then up to his bedroom without saying anything else. I fanned myself as I sat down at the table, hoping that by the time he was back, the tension between us would subside a bit.

It didn't.

The second Sam appeared again at the top of the staircase, I felt as if all the air in the room had been sucked out.

He was wearing shorts and a shirt, but he could very well have forgotten the shirt. He hadn't dried himself properly, so the white fabric was clinging to his skin. His hair was still wet.

"That shower was just what I needed," he said, sitting down at the table. "It woke me up, and I made you blush deliciously."

I looked up from my plate. "Sam!"

"What?" he asked, feigning innocence. "Your voice is stern."

I nodded vigorously. "I feel like we should make a few more things off-limits, but I'm just not sure about the parameters exactly."

"The parameters," he parroted. "Since when did you incorporate business vocabulary in your day-to-day life?"

I groaned. "Since I spent the entire day looking up business lingo for Etsy. I never thought I'd have to start from scratch again, but I have a good feeling about it," I said, digging into my salad. "They do everything different on the site, but I think for my new startup, it's the best way to go."

"I'm very proud of you."

"What for?" I asked him between bites.

"Because not only did you follow your dream, but you lost it, and now you're building it back again."

"I don't really have another choice."

"Yeah, there's always a choice. Most people would just quit."

"That's not an option," I said and left it at that. I couldn't imagine doing anything else. And I also wanted nothing more than to show up my ex-business partner after what she'd done to me. The more I thought about it, the angrier I got, and the more determined I was to succeed.

He flashed me a charming smile. "Look, I talked to my brothers. If you need any sort of help, or business ideas, you can chat with them."

It took me a few seconds to process what he'd said. "You spoke to your brothers about me?"

"Yes. These days, I can't seem to talk to them without mentioning you."

I stretched my legs under the table and accidentally touched his. Goose bumps broke out on my skin as he sucked in a breath.

I cleared my throat. *How can we still react to each other this way after all these years?*

"Why?"

"You know why." He pointed between us. "They predicted this."

"What exactly?" I asked.

"The tension."

I laughed nervously. "Really? So did Alana. I told her she was imagining things."

"That makes two of us. Are we oblivious or what? But we were both wrong, weren't we?" His gaze was trained on me.

I was rooted to my seat. But I couldn't fall prey to those baby blue eyes.

Don't, I chastised myself. *It will not bring anything good. He's probably on the rebound.*

I pointed my fork at him after I ate my last mouthful of salad. "No. I know what's happening. We just need time adjusting."

He cocked a brow, and heat pooled between my legs. Holy shit, my body was reacting weirdly. "You flashing those delicious abs around me is not helping the matter," I continued. "It just spurs my imagination, making me wonder what else you're hiding. Not that I have to wonder, of course. I remember."

He tilted his head playfully. "Would it help if you saw me commando?"

"I walked right into that," I murmured. My heart was beating rapidly. This evening couldn't possibly become more tense.

Luckily, he didn't say anything else as he finished his salad. Afterward, I rose to my feet, but he shook his head. "No, you prepared the meal. I'm cleaning up."

"I made salad from a plastic bag. It was already washed. There wasn't much preparation involved."

"Still, I'm cleaning up." He stood from the table, taking everything at once, putting the plates on top of each other and then the salad bowl. As he grabbed the stack, he accidentally brushed my notebook, and it fell on the floor.

"I got it," he said, putting the stack of dishes back on the table. "Well, well. What do we have here?" he said, slowly rising with his eyes glued to a page that fell out of my notebook.

What could he possibly mean? He probably found my to-do list for the week, but that wasn't terribly exciting.

"You still do pro-and-con lists?"

I gasped. In a fraction of a second, my face felt flaming hot.

He flashed me a purely seductive smile. "You already wrote down that it might be hard to resist my… wait, what is the phrase exactly?"

I took the paper and notebook away from him, putting it on my chair. I didn't just need to fan myself; I wanted to pour a bucket of ice on top of my head. My pulse had gone so haywire that I had trouble hearing properly over the pounding in my ears, but I couldn't miss Sam's voice.

"So, you foresaw some of this trouble even before you moved in?"

He'd called me out on it. No way could I disagree; it was right there in my own handwriting.

I straightened my shoulders. "Why do you think I was hesitating?"

His eyes flashed. "You were right. We do need to identify a few more things as off-limits."

I nodded. "Yeah. I'll try to come up with more, but not tonight."

"Why? Too distracted by my holy hotness?" He smirked.

"Oh shut up."

9

SAM

*S*ome days at the hospital were good. There was no better feeling than saving a patient. Not just saving their life but making their pain go away, or infection, or simply improving their quality of life. It was why I'd gotten into this line of work in the first place. But other days were plain hard. You had losses.

And on days like this, things were really shitty. There'd been a massive accident with thirty patients arriving in the ER. They called me down from peds. All hands had been on deck. Everyone had pulled their weight, and it still hadn't been enough. We'd lost more patients than we saved. This was a bad day for all of us.

The mood in the doctors' lounge was grim. It was crowded. All seats were taken, and a few people were standing against a wall. No one wanted to be alone, not after a day like this; as humans, we processed losses better as a group.

When I first started the job, I used to drive myself crazy going through everything I'd done, wondering what I could've tried. Now I knew better than to do that. What was done was done. I needed my head clear so I could save someone else. Or in this case, I needed to leave what had happened at the door of the hospital so I could relax tonight and be ready to hop back on tomorrow.

It was imperative not to take my losses forward with me. But even though I knew the drill, it was easier said than done.

I was one of the first to leave the doctors' lounge that afternoon. I wasn't on call tonight, and for the first time in many years, I debated actually turning off my phone. It wasn't frowned upon, since I was officially off duty, and I really needed to decompress tonight.

I heard footsteps behind me as I approached the locker room, and I turned around.

"Hey, Sam."

It was Jean. She and I were the same age, but she'd started here after we graduated med school.

"Hey, Jean."

"Look, we all did everything we could today," she said, maybe more for herself than anyone.

I waved my hand. "Let's just leave it at that. All I want is to get out of here and not think about this shitty day."

"Oh, that makes two of us. I plan to go out and get a few drinks."

"Sounds good."

"Do you want to join me? I'm buying."

"I never let a woman buy me drinks."

"Well, if you want to take me out on a date, I won't say no."

I stared at her. *She's asking me out! Fuck me, I must be really out of it if I didn't realize it.* "Jean, no offense, but I'm not in the dating pool."

Her smile fell. "We could go out as colleagues, then."

In theory we could, but I knew better than that. When someone asked you out, they couldn't switch immediately to friend mode or coworker mode.

"I have other plans tonight."

She nodded, turning around and heading in the opposite direction. I was certain she'd intended to go into the locker room to change as well. Now she was avoiding me. Great! This wasn't off to a good start, but we were both professionals. We could overcome any awkwardness if we had to work together.

I took a quick shower, getting out of my scrubs and dressing in jeans and a T-shirt. Decompressing with fellow docs was a normal thing in hospitals, but I didn't want that tonight. I didn't want to go with a group and talk about the day and unpack one another's baggage, telling ourselves that we'd made up what we lost today by saving other people. You never made up for a lost life. You just did your best not to lose more.

I took out my phone and checked my messages, which was one of the first things I did after a shift was over.

Paisley: Uncle Sam, if a boy asks a friend out, can I give him THE TALK, or is it uncool?

I threw my head back, laughing. I loved my niece immensely. How would she even know what "the talk" was?

Sam: Hell yes you can.

Somehow my niece had gotten it into her head that I was the go-to person to ask if something was cool. I had no idea how I'd even gotten myself into that role, but I was going with it.

Paisley: Thank you.

I didn't have any other messages. I put my phone in my back pocket, wondering what to do tonight.

I thought of hanging out with Avery, maybe enjoying a glass of wine, maybe making her blush again.

Energy coiled through me. *Yes!! That's what I want to do tonight.*

We were starting on a dangerous path, but as usual when it came to Avery, I wasn't able to help myself.

I left the hospital a few minutes later, heading straight home. I stopped at the deli down the street that sold Indian food. It was a long shot, but in my experience, once people had a favorite food, it remained their favorite even years later.

Avery had always loved mango chicken. I ordered one for her and a chicken korma for myself. The restaurant owner was an elderly woman. She must have been in her eighties, but she was quick and agile. She reminded me of Gran. I tipped her well when she handed me my order.

I could already feel the tension bleeding from my body, and it wasn't because I was finally going home. It was because Avery was there.

I arrived earlier than usual. Typically after I finished my shift, I went for a run around the hospital campus to get rid of any excess adrenaline. But tonight I wanted to come straight here.

I walked through the inner courtyard and up to the loft. Unlocking the front door, I couldn't get past how much it felt like we were a couple. Most nights, we ate dinner together and caught up about our day.

Back in high school, we'd talked about moving in together once we graduated. It felt ironic that we were doing so sixteen years later… as roommates.

I opened the door wide, stepping inside. Several things clicked at the same time. First, Madonna's "Like a Virgin" was blasting through the loft. Second, Avery was dancing to it. And third, she was buck naked.

I turned hard instantly. I knew I should announce my presence, but I couldn't take my eyes off her. She had the same slender waist as in high school, but her ass had filled out a bit. Her long blonde hair covered her breasts, but it swayed with every move.

"Avery," I said, but it sounded more like a growl, not like her name. I cleared my throat and tried again, louder. "Avery."

She shrieked, spinning around. "Sam." She covered her boobs with one hand and put the other in front of her pussy. I was so hard, it was damn painful. "Alexa, turn off the music." Madonna shut up instantly. "Oh my God, turn around."

Yeah, that would've been the gentlemanly thing to do from

the get-go. But I couldn't think straight. It took all my self-control to turn away. I gripped the edges of the kitchen counter, taking in deep breaths.

"Oh my God. Oh my God. Oh my God," she chanted as she ran up the staircase, probably to her bedroom. "You were supposed to be here in an hour. That's what the schedule on the fridge says."

"I know," I said loudly, trying to think of extremely unpleasant things so my erection would die down. I thought about scalpels, cutting through skin, blood. Nothing helped. Nothing beat that image of Avery dancing naked in the living room. I wouldn't be able to forget that any time soon.

I heard footsteps on the stairs a few minutes later, and I turned around slowly. I couldn't ignore her the whole evening, or avoid looking at her. She was wearing a blue dress, but I still had her naked body imprinted in my brain.

"Sorry about that," she said.

"I thought about surprising you with dinner. I should've given you a heads-up that I'll come earlier."

"Why did you get off sooner?"

"I always finish earlier than what's on the printed schedule. I go for a run, so by the time I get home it's about an hour later."

"After you work for so many hours, you go for a run?" The look on her face was priceless. It was good for me both physically and mentally—it gave me time to mull over the day and put it behind me.

"How do you think the 'holy hotness' gets to exist?"

She lowered her eyes, obviously still uncomfortable about the whole situation.

"Too soon for naked jokes?" I teased.

Her cheeks turned pink. "Oh my God, Sam." She shook her head, closing her eyes.

I had to take a break from making her squirm and blush, no matter how much I liked it; otherwise, I was going to kiss her. In fact, I might do much more than that. I needed to know how her lips felt beneath mine. And that body. Fuck, I needed to touch her.

"I was going to make dinner," she said.

"Salad again?" I chuckled.

"That's why you thought about bringing dinner, didn't you? You hated my salad."

I looked at her, focusing on her vibrant green eyes and not her tempting mouth. "I didn't hate it, just wanted something more substantial. The Indian food down the street looked good. You still like mango chicken?"

"Yes. It's one of my favorites." She looked at the bag behind me on the counter. "You remembered that?"

I grinned. "I remember everything about you, Avery. Everything."

"And yours is still chicken korma?"

Something twisted in my chest. It was like a pressure had suddenly deflated.

"Yeah. Yeah, it is."

She took out the food, putting it on plates. "Want to tell me why your day was so shitty that you didn't even go for a run? Or you don't have to." She probably saw the change of expression on my face.

"I'll just tell you what happened so you know, but I don't want to talk about it."

"Okay."

"There was a massive accident, and everyone was brought to our ER. We lost a lot of patients."

"Oh no. I heard it on the news but didn't realize they were transported to your hospital. They did say the accident was horrific and there were a few deaths on-site. The expressway is still closed. Oh, Sam, I'm so sorry."

"Getting over a loss doesn't get easier. And this was plural. A lot of people died at the hospital." My mind wouldn't let go as it played a video of the ER scene; it was massive and dreadful, to say the least.

"I'm guessing you wanted to just relax and sleep tonight?"

"Yes and no. I just wanted to take my mind off it, which you did brilliantly with your sexy dance." And there I went again, making her blush. I couldn't help myself. But coming home to a naked Avery was just what the doctor ordered. Pun intended.

I wanted to lean in and check exactly how far down her dress that blush went. It spread on her neck and the part of her chest the fabric didn't cover.

She smiled slightly. "If it was for a good cause, then I'm not feeling as embarrassed about it."

"You shouldn't be embarrassed at all. Your dancing is on point, as usual, and you're so fucking sexy, Avery. Your body is perfect, as far as I can see."

She looked me straight in the eyes, jutting her chin forward and clearing her throat. "Sam."

"You're using your boundaries voice, Avery, but you haven't set any."

"That's because every week we seem to break every boundary known to mankind. Seems like a waste of time to set any. Now let's eat, and while we do that, I'll brainstorm ways to distract you this evening."

"I suggest dancing."

She grinned. "Don't start again."

"Hey, I didn't say anything about naked dancing, but glad to know your mind went straight there."

She narrowed her eyes before taking a spoonful of food. I was damn hungry too. It had been a long while since I'd had my last meal.

"This is very good," she murmured. "I remember the shop now. It's literally down the street. Two blocks away."

"Yeah, the one with the elderly lady at the counter," I confirmed.

"Do they have delivery as well?"

"I didn't ask, but you can tell me whenever you're in the mood for it. It's on my way from the hospital anyway."

She nodded, eating with huge gulps. She finished eating before I did.

"I'm glad this is still your favorite dish," I said. "I was hoping I'd made the right choice."

"I was famished," she admitted. "And I have a few ideas about distracting you."

"Does it include dancing?"

She sighed. "There's no winning with you."

I shook my head, laughing. "Nope. So, what do you have in mind?"

SAM

a very didn't miss a beat. She seemed to have the night planned. "I was thinking more like a bottle of wine, although I think this has already escalated to whiskey level. And we can definitely put on some music, as long as you promise, one, to stop with the innuendos, and two... Hmm, I have to think about the second boundary. I need to make it a good one."

She was adorable, and I played along. "You can have as many boundaries as you want."

"No, no. You seem to have trouble keeping track of them," she said with sass. "Best to limit the number. Maybe then you'll remember them. I can make us some kick-ass cocktails, if you want. We have Coke and bourbon. It was in one of the boxes your brothers carried in."

"Okay. I haven't drunk Jack and Coke in a while."

"It's not fashionable anymore, is it?" she asked.

"Honestly, I've been gone for so long that I have no clue what drinks are *in*."

"Gin. It's popular, and I love it. But we don't have any."

"I'll order some if you like it," I countered.

"You don't have to order it for me," she said.

Why was she surprised that I wanted to do something for her?

She jumped up from the table, about to take her plate, when I scolded, "No, sit. I'm cleaning up."

"But I didn't cook."

"You're making cocktails." I winked at her.

I cleaned up everything while she busied herself taking out the drinks and mixing them expertly.

"You're doing it professionally," I remarked.

"I worked as a bartender for a while when I was in community college. I also waitressed."

"How many jobs did you have, exactly?"

She laughed, but it was devoid of humor. "Who can keep track? I took everything that came my way, and it was still impossible to keep up with bills."

"Why didn't you tell me? I would've helped."

She stopped putting ice cubes in the drinks and looked up at me. "I know you would have. That's why I didn't tell you."

"That makes no sense."

"Oh, Sam. Let's not get into it tonight."

"You promise we'll talk about it another time?"

"What if we never do? That sounds like a great plan."

I swallowed hard, moving closer to her, putting a hand on the counter and the other at the small of her back.

She straightened up abruptly, as if an electric current rushed through her. I was very close, but she wasn't making any attempt to move away or put distance between us. Her perfume was damn intoxicating.

"I always wondered why you left like that," I said softly. "Why you kept me out of your life."

She turned her head to look straight at me. Her breath was shaky. "Sam, it wasn't like that. I didn't want to cut you out. I didn't even want to leave. I just had to." She swallowed hard. "And I didn't want you to get bogged down with everything. Let's not sour the mood, okay?"

She handed me a glass.

"Want to go out on the balcony?" I suggested.

"Sure. But I'm going to need a cozy blanket. It's cold."

"What's with the coffee cup?" I pointed to the empty cup next to the bottle of Jack.

"I used it to measure the alcohol. I'm not sure if I got the ratio right, but we'll see, I guess."

I took the "cozy blankets," as she called them, from the couch, and we went on the balcony, where there were two chairs overlooking the crowded street. The building in front of us was full of colorful murals. Jazz music played from a corner down the street. We sat in the chairs, clinked glasses, and started sipping. She seemed utterly relaxed, wrapping herself up in the blankets, eyes closed, smiling contentedly.

We both drank our cocktails in silence—maybe a bit too fast. I'd emptied my glass before I knew it, and so had she.

"This is so blissful."

"It really is. I haven't had this feeling in years," I said.

She blinked her eyes open. "What do you mean?"

"Just being home and relaxing."

"I imagine the pace is different in Doctors Without Borders."

"Yes. Especially because at first I was in areas with lots of conflicts."

She tensed. "Were you ever hurt?"

I shook my head. "Nothing really bad. I once got a stray bullet in my left leg."

She gasped. "Oh my God."

"I took it out myself pretty quickly. I wasn't left with any permanent nerve damage or anything."

She looked at my left leg, and I cocked a brow. "Want to see proof?"

"Maybe."

"What a creative way to tell me to take off my clothes."

She laughed softly. "I know it's noble and everything, but

74

wow, going to an unstable area is something. When did you move to Honduras?"

"When I started having a relationship with another doctor here in Chicago. I moved to Honduras so I could fly home more often. There are more direct flights to Chicago from there."

She nodded and asked, "Did she visit you?"

"No. Wouldn't even meet me halfway for a vacation. That should've been a clue, but it didn't sink in. I just assumed she was busy. To be fair, she was. Her schedule looked pretty much the way mine is now."

Avery nodded. "Is she working with you now?"

"No, she's at a different hospital."

"Okay."

I shook my head. "Damn, I usually don't talk so much. How much alcohol is in this, exactly? It feels strong, but I haven't had a Jack and Coke in years, so I'm not sure I remember how it's supposed to taste."

Avery frowned. "I don't know either, to be honest, but I don't think it's that strong. Want me to make another one?"

"Sure."

She rose to her feet, dropping the blankets to the floor.

"Whoa." She lost her balance, gripping the door with both hands.

"Are you okay?" I jumped out of my chair, intending to steady her. Instead, I realized I was having huge balance issues of my own. The floor seemed to tilt at a ninety-degree angle before it corrected itself. I grabbed the other edge of the door for support and put a hand on her back.

She leaned into my touch. "I guess they were pretty strong, huh?" she murmured.

"Yeah," I replied. "How about some water?"

"Good idea."

"Careful. There's a step down from the terrace," I said.

"I know."

I put both hands on her waist from behind, guiding her. Why I thought I was in any position to keep her safe, I had no idea, but every instinct told me to try anyway. We walked slowly in a straight line until we reached the kitchen counter.

"Oh God," she said, looking at the cup.

"What?"

"I messed up. I should've added another measure of Coke. We're going to be so out of it tomorrow."

"I don't have a shift," I said immediately.

I filled us each a glass of water from the tap. She was leaning against the kitchen counter and immediately grabbed the glass, drinking with huge gulps. So huge, in fact, that water spilled out from the sides of her mouth and straight onto her dress, making it transparent.

"Oops," she murmured, setting the glass down. Then she noticed her dress. She grinned, covering the see-through patch above her right breast with her palm.

I was semihard already. This was insane.

"How do I keep making a mess of things around you?" she asked. "You make me nervous."

"I don't want that. I don't want you to be uncomfortable."

"I didn't say uncomfortable, Sam. Just nervous. I thought this would be easier."

I moved closer to her. I shouldn't have, but I did. I put my hand on the other side of the counter. If I pressed myself just an inch closer to her, our bodies would be touching.

"What? Living with me?"

"Yes. So much time has passed that I thought we'd be perfect strangers. Back then, you know, I didn't want to leave," she murmured.

I looked her straight in the eyes. "Then why did you?"

She shrugged. "I was head over heels in love with you. I thought... I thought you were the one."

Fuck. The confession was like a punch to my gut. "So, why did you leave?" I insisted.

"Because you had so many plans. To go to college and go to med school and join Doctors Without Borders. And when I heard of Mom's illness, I knew that for the next few years, I'd be bogged down with trips to the doctor and worries. And I didn't want that to weigh on you."

"It wouldn't have weighed on me. That is not who I am. You know that. I would've been there for you every step of the way."

"While trying to make the grades for med school? You can't know that." She ran a hand through her hair, biting her lower lip. "It doesn't matter anyway. What's done is done. I figured… well, I guess I figured back then that if you really wanted us to be together, you would've reached out somehow."

I brought my hand to her jaw, turning it until we were making eye contact again. "You made it clear you didn't want that, so I didn't. No matter how much I wanted to come after you."

"You did?" she whispered.

"Yes. Fuck yes." I ran my thumb over her lips.

She shuddered, moaning against my skin. The reverberation went straight to my cock. I cupped her cheek, and she clasped my wrist.

"Sam, don't… or I'll let you kiss me." She was shaking slightly.

I rested my forehead on her temple. My lips brushed her cheek near her ear. "Why shouldn't I?"

She didn't reply right away, and we spent the next few seconds in silence. I was waiting for her to gather her thoughts. I desperately wanted to kiss her, but I wouldn't do so until she gave me the green light in no uncertain terms. I was drunk as hell, but I still needed her to clearly say yes.

I squeezed the kitchen counter more forcefully. I needed to kiss her more than I needed to breathe right now, but she still wasn't giving me the okay.

"Sam, please," she muttered, and I moved away. It was the only logical thing I could do. Being near her was physically difficult.

"I think we had too much to drink," she said.

"We can agree on that," I replied. "I'm going to bed."

"It's nine o'clock."

"We're going to need all the sleep we can get. And water."

"And aspirin."

"I don't have any," I said automatically. "I usually just take what I need when I go to the hospital."

"I don't have any either." She pouted.

"Come on. I'll help you up to bed. You're worse off than I am."

"But why? I made the same drink for both of us."

"I have about forty pounds on you."

"Forty pounds of super-sexy muscles." To my astonishment, she came closer and put her hand on my right arm, squeezing. "Yeah. It's just as hard as I imagined."

I groaned at her touch.

She looked up at me and immediately dropped her hand. "I can't believe I did that."

"I'll give you a pass since you're so drunk. Now come on, off to bed with you." With one hand on her shoulder, I turned her around and put my other hand on her waist, guiding her.

"Ooh, bossy Sam is sexy."

"Woman, stop drunk flirting with me. I'm hanging on by a thread as it is," I teasingly said, even though it was the truth.

She hiccupped. "Great. Now I'm embarrassing myself. This isn't fair. You drank the same thing, and there's still nothing embarrassing about you."

I carefully helped her up the stairs to her bedroom so both of us wouldn't tumble back down. She might be further gone than I was but not by much.

From behind her, I brought my lips to her ear. "So, want to know something that's super embarrassing?"

"Yes, please. Even the scales."

"I've been hard for you this entire evening, ever since I came in and saw you dancing. It's subsided in the meantime, but now it's back in force since our conversation at the counter."

I felt her knees buckle, and then she pressed her thighs together.

Realization hit me. My words made her wet. She was driving me insane.

"Sam, it's all or nothing with you, huh?"

"Yes," I agreed.

Letting go of her, I pulled back her covers. She sat down on the bed and said, "Okay, I'm good now. Thanks very much. You can go, and I'll take off my clothes. I can do that on my own."

"No worries. I wasn't going to offer any help," I said, knowing I couldn't damn well handle that.

I walked to the door with determined strides. When I was in the doorway, she said, "Sam, can we please not talk about what we talked about tonight tomorrow?"

I turned around. "That only half made sense, but I got the message."

"Thank you." She sounded genuinely relieved.

"Good night, Avery."

As I headed to my room, I knew I wasn't going to fall asleep any time soon. I needed a cold shower first.

AVERY

"*W*hy are there drummers in my room?" I cried the next morning. "And a flashlight?" I pulled the covers over my head.

Boy, did I overindulge last night or what?

"That's the sunlight, and the drumming sound is your alarm clock," Sam said from somewhere nearby.

"I'm pretty sure the whole street has heard it by now." I pushed away the covers, immediately turning off the clock. I blinked hard, looking around. "What time is it? Eight o'clock in the morning? No way. We slept almost twelve hours."

"No, *you* slept twelve hours. I woke up two hours ago and went for a run. Your alarm clock went off a couple minutes ago. Since you weren't budging, I came to turn it off."

"Am I the only one who's got a hammering headache? How did you even have the energy to go running?"

"I had a headache too. Decided to literally walk it off."

That was when I realized he was holding a glass with a yellow drink. He set it on the nightstand next to me.

"It will help with the headache and any nausea. It's got a lot of ginger. I went out this morning and bought all the ingredients."

"You had one too?"

"Yeah, it really helped."

"Oh my God. This is the hangover cure your mom never knew about, right?"

He nodded. "You've got a good memory."

Back in high school, he told me his grandmother prepped him and his brothers this drink whenever they came home from a party. She'd never told her daughter-in-law they were hungover, just that they needed a tonic.

After I drank it, I finally pushed myself up from bed. Sam was looking at me intently, as if he expected me to tumble any second.

"No, my balance is quite good," I assured him.

"Great. Then I'm going to wait for you in the living room with breakfast."

I jerked my head back. "You made breakfast?"

"Sure. It's my day off. Why not?"

"I don't know. I figured you'd have stuff to do."

"I have plenty to do later, but I thought I'd start the day by having breakfast with you." There was a playful glint in his eyes.

What exactly happened last night? Then I remembered the naked dance. *My God, I've only been living with this man for two weeks and he's already seen me naked.*

After he left, I changed into a dress and quickly brushed my teeth. I was going to shower after he headed out for the day; I didn't want to leave him waiting. My hair was a mess, so I just gathered it up in a ponytail and called it a day.

When I came out into the living room, wafts of delicious aromas surrounded me. My stomach was rumbling. That drink was truly magic, because only a couple minutes before, I thought my head would hurt the whole day and I'd have no appetite. Neither of those things could be further from the truth now.

To be fair, I probably would've gotten a hell of an appetite just from seeing Sam in the kitchen. He looked surreal in his white T-shirt and jeans, like he didn't belong there at all. Then again, I didn't think he belonged in a hospital either. Those scrubs covered up far too much. He should be on the cover of magazines and on posters. In high school, I secretly thought he might become a movie star or something. He certainly had the looks—his vivid blue eyes contrasted beautifully with his dark hair, and his tanned complexion made his eyes pop. But he'd followed his heart and became a doctor.

I headed straight to the kitchen island. The second I put my hands on the cool granite counter, memories from last night flooded me. *Oh my God.* I remembered us standing near the sink. I'd gulped down water and confessed all my deepest secrets.

Had I imagined that? It could be. Over the years, I'd often wondered what I would do if I saw Sam again. If I'd tell him why I left him high and dry and seemingly never looked back. His mouth had been so close to my ear and my cheek. Instantly, I remembered the burning feeling on my skin where his lips grazed me. I definitely hadn't imagined that.

I swallowed hard, trying to sort through the memories and decide what had actually happened.

"What are you thinking about?" He'd taken his focus off the pan and was staring at me.

"Deciding if I should try what you're cooking or not," I said. "I don't want to risk food poisoning. Though I hardly think you can do that with sunny-side ups."

He flashed me a panty-melting smile. My pajama bottoms nearly fell to the floor all by themselves. "Hey, I ate your salad. It's an unspoken rule between roommates to eat each other's cooking."

My body buzzed from his words. He hadn't even meant it as an innuendo—or had he? I was still so busy trying to discern what happened last night that I couldn't focus on what was going on right now.

He glanced at my cheeks, and I realized I was blushing. *Well, this day is off to a good start.*

"What's that look for?"

"I don't know. I'm just lost in thought," I said, trying to regain my faculties. I swallowed hard, taking in his body language.

Mischievous glint, on point.

Charming smile, very on point.

Overall smug expression, through the roof.

I had no choice but to ask him; otherwise, I would obsess about this the whole day.

"Sam, is there anything you'd like to tell me?"

That playful glint in his eyes turned smoldering. "About what?"

"I don't know. You tell me." I crossed my legs, standing straighter, suddenly feeling sassy.

He chuckled while he took the pan off the stove and put the eggs on two plates. Then he garnished them with sliced tomatoes and avocado.

Wow. I hadn't seen this side of Sam before. The man was thorough. He put the two plates down and sat on the chair next to me.

"Sam, what are you doing?"

"Buying time," he replied easily.

"You need more time before you answer my question?"

He turned around, facing me, and I did the same. The insides of his thighs were touching the outsides of my mine. The contact zinged through me. I sucked in a breath, darting my tongue out and wetting my lower lip. It suddenly felt dry. Sam's gaze was fixed on my mouth. My body started to shake slightly.

"The thing is, Avery, you asked me not to remind you."

"My God, I did?"

"Yeah, and I promised. And as you know, I'm nothing if not a man of my word."

I couldn't believe it. That meant I definitely spilled some secrets last night.

I couldn't look away from him. Our gazes were locked. I also couldn't bring myself to restart that conversation, so instead I shifted in my seat, turning around so I faced my plate. I immediately dug in, eating a mouthful of egg, half a slice of avocado, and half a cherry tomato.

"This is great," I said. "Very nourishing."

"I'm glad you approve."

Even without looking, I knew he hadn't shifted positions, so he was still looking at me, waiting. My heart rate accelerated. I felt his presence intensely. The wall between us was full of sexy tension, but it was still a wall in my head. I had reasons for keeping the structure in place. I was the one who left, yes, and I broke my own heart in the process too. But I wasn't ready to open that old wound. It had never healed. I still had the scabs to prove it, and I didn't want to pick at them.

A few seconds later, he turned his focus to his plate, and I felt I could breathe a little more easily.

"What are you doing today?" he asked as we both enjoyed our breakfast.

"I'll work on my Etsy store and beg a few factories to work with me. My stock is running low. After that, I promised Alana that I'd take her out for drinks. I want to treat her to thank her for being a good friend and letting me camp on her couch."

"So Alana gets special treatment, but I don't."

"Apparently you get plenty of special treatment. And you repay me by using unorthodox ways to fish confessions from me. Which you don't even want to share."

"Avery."

Oh God. He'd said my name in a low whisper, along with a groan. The sound made my panties combust.

"First of all," he continued, "you were the one making the cocktails."

Oh, that's right. I remember. So I set myself up. "True, I can't blame you for that." I turned around. Big mistake. I hadn't realized he'd leaned in, and now we were much too close. I could see the gray flecks in his blue eyes. The last time I was this close to him, we were together in high school. "I can still put a little bit of blame on you."

He cocked a brow, smirking. "How come?"

"You've got all this charming sexiness going on. It's hard to keep my mind straight."

"Right." He narrowed his eyes. "And as to the confession, I can tell you. You only have to ask."

There was an awkward pause. Clearly he was waiting for me to ask him to break his word, but I just shook my head. My heart was hammering against my rib cage again. No, once we'd openly discussed that, things between us would shift. Right now, we could pretend last night had been a drunken slip between friends and nothing more.

"No. I made you promise, so I must have had a good reason for it," I said as I hopped down from my chair.

Sam did the same.

"What are you doing?" I asked him.

"I'm making you coffee."

I jerked my head back. "How do you know I was about to do that?"

"You've been eyeing that coffee machine almost as much as you've been eyeing me. I don't like to read into things, but I'm going to take the hint that it means you really want coffee. More than you want me."

The tips of my breasts turned to hard nubs. I wasn't even going to wonder about that. My body and my brain clearly weren't working in sync today.

We both approached the coffee machine. I leaned against the kitchen sink and immediately remembered being in the exact same position last night. Sam had whispered in my ear, and I'd begged him not to kiss me, even though I had wanted it so badly. God, I still wanted it now. I glanced at him out of the corner of my eye and saw him looking at me intently. Was he thinking about those moments as well?

And then, all of a sudden, I remembered all my confessions.

"Sam," I murmured. He exhaled sharply. "I'm sorry about last night. I shouldn't have blurted everything out."

His Adam's apple bobbed up and down. "I wanted you to tell me. I wanted to know. I've wondered so often where things went wrong. Why you wanted to end things. The real reason why you left."

"I never wanted you to think it was your fault." I could smell his shower gel, so fresh and clean. "You still use Nivea Men Fresh Ocean?" It brought back many vivid memories of him.

"I switched back to it recently," he replied with a grin.

He smelled so good. I sniffed him. I actually *sniffed* him. Then I leaned in even closer and brought my nose to his neck.

He groaned again, and then his mouth was on mine. I'd never felt anything like this before in my life. It was like he was kissing me for the first time, and yet it also felt like he'd never stopped. He knew what I liked, and he'd always been a great kisser. But now? Now he was perfect. His lips moved with precision. His hands were all over my body, on my upper thigh and my waist. Then one of them moved to my lower back, pressing me against his abdomen, which, yes, was as hard as I'd imagined.

I was melting in his arms. I put my palms on his shoulders as his right hand brushed back down my upper thigh. On instinct, I lifted my leg, wrapping it around him.

He groaned against my mouth, and the reverberations shook my body. Then he slid his hands under my ass and lifted me onto the counter. I was towering over him now, but I liked this angle. He kissed me until I was so turned on that there was no way he could mistake the tremors in my body. I pressed my thighs against the sides of his torso. I needed friction. God, I needed this man so badly.

He kissed from my mouth up to my ear.

"Avery," he groaned. "Fuck, how I missed this."

He fisted my hair, tilting my head to one side and kissing my neck.

"Sam," I whispered. My voice was shaky, just like my body.

I curled my hands over his shoulders, tugging at his shirt. I moved closer to the edge of the counter, spreading my thighs wide. He pushed me slightly backward, and I gasped as a small explosion went through me.

Holy fuck. Did I just have a mini orgasm from pressing myself against the ridge of his jeans?

Abruptly, he pulled back. I blinked, confused, straightening up too. He looked at me intently and touched my face with the back of his fingers, feathering them down my chin and then the side of my neck. His eyes were on my lips.

"I want you, Avery. So damn bad. I want to keep kissing you. I want to make you come. I want to sink inside you."

I was done for. Every rational thought left my brain.

"I want you too," I admitted.

He dragged his eyes up to glance at me. "But I won't do any of that."

"Why not?" I sounded desperate, but I had no shame.

"Because last night, you begged me not to kiss you. Not to even remind you of our conversation." His voice was suddenly hard. "I don't want us to do something you'll regret."

I shifted on the cold granite counter, suddenly feeling out of sorts and uncomfortable and completely vulnerable in front of him.

He took a huge step to the right, reaching for the counter, gripping it tightly with one hand. I had a strange sensation that it was all he could do not to come right back here and kiss me. If I tempted him enough, he might. My body certainly demanded it. I hadn't even known I'd missed him so much. But I knew he was right—it was too soon, and I didn't want us to regret anything.

"I'm so embarrassed right now," I murmured.

"There's no reason for that."

I hopped off the counter, tugging at the hem of my shirt for no reason.

"You're looking at me with a wicked smile again," I stated.

"Yes, I am."

"You're not even denying it."

"Why should I, Avery? I'm an open book."

"I'm not sure where we go from here. How do we forget about what just happened?"

"We don't," Sam said nonchalantly.

"But you just said—"

"That I don't plan to make you come right here, right now. Not that I don't plan to do it in the future."

My entire body instantly heated up.

"Wh-What?" I stuttered.

"You're not ready. So I'm going to lay the groundwork. Find out exactly what's holding you back and dismantle every single wall you have."

I was too stunned to reply.

Judging by his smug smile, Sam was clearly enjoying my reaction. This was a completely new side of him. The boy I'd left hadn't been smug. Well, the boy I'd left hadn't even been a dirty talker, so he'd definitely changed in that department. I liked it.

What other changes would I like?

None, Avery. Absolutely none, a voice said at the back of my mind. *Focus on getting your life back on track and that's it. Falling for Sam Maxwell shouldn't even be part of that plan.*

A loud sound rang through the living room. Sam dropped his chin to his chest.

"What's the matter?" I asked.

"That's a ringtone I have for the hospital. It means they need me back."

"But this is your day off," I said indignantly.

"I know. I should've shut off my phone. Now that I'm available, I can't ignore it." He walked to the couch, grabbing his phone and putting it to his ear. "Hi. Yes. And there's no one else who can do it? Fine, I'll be there in a few minutes." That was it. He hung up the phone.

"You're going to work now?" I asked. "But last night you were completely exhausted."

"Thanks to your Jack and Coke, I had a solid twelve hours of sleep. That's almost double my usual. Damn, I was going to take today to think about everything I want to do to you," he murmured. "In which order and when."

I swallowed hard. This day had taken an unbelievable turn.

"And now you'll be busy," I said. "So I guess you'll pencil it in at another time?" Surely if he could be so nonchalant about it, I could be too. Granted, I had to work on my dirty talk so I could put him just as on edge as he put me.

He smirked. "Nah, I'll keep it in mind the whole time. Maybe I'll even figure it out for this evening."

AVERY

"You don't have to spend all your money on me!" Alana protested. The bar was loud. She had to lean into me so I could hear anything at all.

"Not all my money," I assured her. "But I wanted to treat you. If you hadn't offered to take me in, I probably wouldn't be here today."

"Why did you order a nonalcoholic cocktail for yourself?" she asked suspiciously as the bartender slipped the drinks toward us. I shrugged, but didn't reply.

We clinked glasses, and I looked around for a cozy spot where we could talk, but it wasn't likely to happen.

"Let's go outside," I said and we made our way through the crowd slowly, careful not to slosh our drinks.

On the way out, I noticed a few party girls were already inebriated. I *so* didn't want that to be me tonight. Once outside, I took a deep breath, and we stepped sideways to the corner of the building. Unfortunately, I smelled cigarettes in the air, but we were trying to find a place sheltered from the wind. I'd forgotten how cold November was in Chicago.

She narrowed her eyes at me. "Hey, you look guilty. Well, not guilty, but like you did something you weren't supposed to."

I bit my lip. Some things truly didn't change. She could read me like a book, just like back in high school.

"It's about Sam, isn't it?"

I rolled my shoulders. "How can you tell?"

"Experience."

"Well, first, let's start with why no alcohol. Last night, I made us Jack and Cokes, and I made a mistake when I measured the Jack."

"You had sex with him," Avery accused.

"No! I might have told him a few things I shouldn't have, and we nearly kissed, but no sex."

She waved her hand, taking a sip of her drink. "I thought you had something juicier to tell me."

"I do."

She let go of the straw and looked straight at me. "Okay."

"This morning… well, one thing led to another, and we kissed. It was a *very* hot kiss."

"Did it lead to more?"

"Not exactly. He says I'm not ready. It's all very confusing."

"Not to me," Alana said.

"Oh really? Enlighten me, then."

"I don't know if I should. I don't want to influence your train of thought."

I laughed, sipping from my virgin margarita. "We're not in high school anymore, Alana."

Just then, my phone started vibrating.

"And what's that vibrating?" she asked. "You got a dildo in your pants?"

"Don't be silly. It's my phone."

"Close," Alana said when she saw Sam's name on the screen.

I shook my head at her. "You're unbelievable."

"I know, right?"

"You're even more shameless than in high school."

"I get better with age. Speaking of which, how are Sam's kissing skills?"

"Very much improved," I said. The phone call went to voice mail, but then I noticed he'd also sent me a few messages.

"What does he say?"

Alana hovering over my shoulder while we were obsessing over Sam's texts literally gave me flashbacks from our teen years.

Sam: Hey, gorgeous. How was your day?

"Hmm, you've progressed to 'gorgeous' already. I approve," Alana said.

"You know what? Finish your drink and stay away from my phone."

"But best friend privileges include snooping. Even when you're an adult."

Sam: What are you doing tonight? There's this amazing street food festival taking place if you're still into it.

"Oh, he remembered that about you!" she exclaimed.

"Alana! No snooping."

"Okay, okay. I'm on my best behavior. Look, I'm taking a step back." She sipped her drink, looking at me expectantly.

Avery: I'm out with Alana having drinks, remember?

Sam: I forgot. Enjoy your girls evening, then. I won't be in your way. I'll put my master plan in motion another time. Say hi to Alana for me. Is she still a fan of me?

I laughed.

Avery: Yes she is.

Sam: Good. Then she's going to do some of that ground-work for me already. This is working out perfectly.

Avery: You're awfully confident, Sam.

Sam: Always. Enjoy your evening. We can talk more when you're home.

I had a light buzz going even though I was having a nonalcoholic cocktail. Was I drunk on Sam already? The man wasn't even here.

"You know what? This *is* just like high school," Alana said. "You're blushing when Sam's texting you. And he still knows how to push your buttons."

"Oh yeah, he's a master at it."

"So what's holding you back?" She ran her hand through her gorgeous mane of hair, untangling some of the strands. She'd always had this messy hairstyle on purpose, even when we were younger. She didn't brush it often because it became too frizzy. It looked effortlessly beautiful on her.

"My life is in shambles, Alana. I'm up to my eyeballs in debt. It's hard to find a job because I was a jack-of-all-trades and ran my own business for the past five years. I'm doing logo design gigs on Fiverr to keep afloat. I had to move in with a roommate to afford an apartment in Chicago. I feel like the last thing I need right now is to have a man in my life in any way, shape, or form."

"Well, news flash: you already have one living with you."

"I know, but it's not the same."

"And you kissed him."

"Thank you for reminding me."

She snorted. "My point is, I think everything is already complicated. You might as well just roll with it."

I shook my head, taking another sip of the margarita. I should've bought one with alcohol after all.

"You know what they say about best-laid plans."

I frowned. "No. What?"

"If the best-laid plans don't work, then at least get laid."

I burst out laughing, accidentally snorting margarita through my nose, making us both laugh harder.

"I've never heard that saying before."

She nodded. "I just came up with it, but it's one for the books, isn't it?"

* * *

ALANA and I stayed out on the town for another few hours before I headed home. It was a chilly evening, but it was nice for a walk, so I didn't head straight to the loft, just wandered through our neighborhood, soaking it all up.

My phone beeped as I stopped in front of a particularly gorgeous mural depicting a woman holding her baby in one arm. I took it out and looked at the screen. I didn't know the number, but that was very exciting. It could be one of the seemingly hundreds of factories I'd contacted this week.

Without hesitation, I answered. "Hi, this is Avery."

"Hi, Avery. I'm Jack Dempsey from Dempsey Productions." His voice was brusque.

"Hi, Mr. Dempsey," I said. I couldn't remember exactly which factory that was, but it didn't matter.

"You're in Chicago, right?"

"Yes, exactly."

"Okay. Listen, I like your designs, but I need a very detailed spec as well as a production plan." He spoke very fast, and I was more than grateful that I hadn't had any real cocktails. I could barely keep things straight as it was.

"I can make one. When do you need it?"

"Why don't you send it by Wednesday of next week? I'll email you the address."

"All right."

"I won't keep you any longer. Have a great evening."

That's it? I thought he'd want to chat for a bit so we could get to know each other better.

"Wait. Can we also schedule a longer call?" I pressed. "I'd like to know more about you and your company."

"Sure. Let's chat next Wednesday after I get your presentation."

I sighed. Then again, perhaps it was better to wait until after I sent him the specs. If he didn't like them, we'd just waste each other's time.

"Sounds good. You'll get my presentation by then."

He seemed in a hurry. Perhaps he had more potential clients to talk to this evening. I was so excited that I was tempted to call Alana again for a celebratory drink.

"No, no, no, Avery. Don't jinx yourself. Besides, you've wasted enough money on drinks. Time to get down to work."

I headed straight back home even though I had so much energy that I could circle the block a few times more. But it was late, and though this was a nice neighborhood, I couldn't be too careful.

I'd expected the loft to be completely dark when I arrived, but to my astonishment, Sam was still awake. He was sitting on the couch with a laptop. Judging by the amount of light on his face, I assumed he was watching a movie or something.

"Hey," I said.

He immediately set the laptop aside, but the screen kept flashing, and I caught a few sentences. He was watching something medical.

"How was your evening?" he asked.

"Amazing. And guess what happened on the way back to the loft? I got a call from a factory owner who's interested in working with me. I've got a few days to put together a plan."

"Congrats."

"Thanks." I blushed. *Oh my goodness.* "Sooo for the next week, you're not allowed to distract me."

He watched me intently, then nodded. "Okay. For one week straight, I'm not going to distract you at all."

"And after that?" I inquired.

The corners of his mouth lifted. "No more promises after that."

* * *

Over the next few days, I buckled down, working on the presentation and my Fiverr gigs. To my astonishment, Sam kept his word. He was gone most of the time, of course, but even when he was home, he was on his best behavior.

"Avery," he said a few days later, in the evening.

"Mm?" I didn't look at him, just kept tapping away at my computer. Then a whiff of something delicious reached my nose.

He pushed a plate of chicken dasheri in front of me.

My eyes widened. "Whoa, where did this come from?"

"I bought it. You need to eat."

"Yes, sir. Yes."

His eyes flashed, and his nostrils flared.

Okay, I don't want to know what just went through his mind. I had a few ideas, but I didn't need them confirmed. "Are you going to eat with me?"

"I already did in the kitchen. I didn't want to disturb you."

"Sam, you wouldn't be disturbing me."

"Let me correct that—*distract* you. I'm doing my best to keep my word, Avery."

"Thanks for that."

I pushed my laptop away and started eating. It was nine o'clock, so I could probably call it a day anyway.

A vibrating noise made me aware that my phone was ringing somewhere in the room.

"That's mine. I don't know where I put it," I said, looking around.

"It's on the kitchen counter," Sam said, grabbing it. "Hey, it's your mom. Here you go." He stretched his hand toward me, but then we both heard Mom's voice.

Sam's eyebrows rose. "I might have accidentally accepted the call." Then he grinned, putting my phone to his ear.

I jumped to my feet.

"Good evening," he said in his most charming tone.

"Sam!" I heard Mom exclaim. "How are you doing?"

"I was just about to hand the phone to Avery. She's fine. Working even more than me this week."

I rolled my eyes. "That's not possible."

"I'm trying to take care of her, make sure she eats and doesn't exhaust herself. How are you, Mrs. Sinclair?" He smiled, and it was genuine. "That's good to know. Okay, I'll give Avery the phone. She's throwing daggers at me with her eyes."

I snatched the phone from him. "Hey, Mom," I said, walking a few feet away.

"Darling, you're going to burn out."

Mom was always afraid of that. I'd had a few burnouts while I was trying to hold things together when she was sick. She knew me too well.

"Don't worry. I have a tight deadline this week, and I'm determined to make it work. Then I'll relax."

"You ignored my calls yesterday, sweetie. Are you sure everything's okay?"

"Oh my God, I did? I didn't even realize that. I'm sorry."

"See what I mean? Don't overdo it, honey."

"How are you feeling, Mom? Your checkup is coming soon, right? Don't forget about it."

She'd been sick with lymphoma all those years ago, and though she was considered completely healthy after five years, she still did bloodwork checkups twice a year.

"Yes. Don't you worry about that. Now tell me, how is living with Sam?"

I glanced up at the man. He had his eyes trained on me.

"It's nice," I said, looking for a neutral word. Something that wouldn't give too much away.

"Is he still the same great guy he was back then?"

"I assume so, yes."

"Hmm... Put him back on the phone," she ordered.

"What?"

"I need to talk to him."

"You need to talk to Sam?"

Sam grinned like a Cheshire cat.

"Yes, darling. That's what I just said."

"Why?"

"That's between me and him."

I couldn't believe this. He strode right to me, taking my phone. After listening, then responding a couple times—"Yeah, sure. Of course, ma'am. It will be my pleasure."—he ended the call.

What the heck is going on? I looked at him suspiciously. "What did Mom want with you?"

"I can't say." He paused, then said, "Oh, she gives you her love and says she'll call again later this week."

"Oh come on, Sam. Don't play that game with me."

He shrugged, leaning against the kitchen island. "It's not a game. She made me promise. You know I like to keep my word."

13

AVERY

*O*ver the next few days, I worked tirelessly on the presentation. I kept working on Fiverr gigs on the side. It wasn't terribly exciting. People asked for basic logo designs, but that was fine by me.

I also spent more time than I should on my would-be Etsy store, discovering keywords to improve algorithms, making my products easy for customers to find, and designing more merchandise. I was getting ahead of myself—deep down, I knew that. Even quick-production batches could take up to a few months. But I was determined to be positive about this.

I made sure every detail was perfect in the presentation.

I'd drawn up several of these over the course of my business, and I was confident I was doing a good job. My sister, Jamie, offered to take a look at it as well, and on Wednesday at 7:00 a.m., I was waiting on pins and needles for her answer.

Her email came in at 7:05 a.m. I was supposed to send it to Jack at nine o'clock.

Jamie: You're a pro. The numbers look good. Go get him!
Avery: Thanks, Jamie.

I emailed Jack the next second. From that point on, I

pretended to work on more designs, but honestly, I couldn't really focus.

At 11:00 a.m., he replied, asking if we could chat at 6:00 p.m. my time. *Crap.* Seven more hours of biting my nails was going to be the end of me, but there wasn't anything I could do, so I agreed. Then I messaged Sam to let him know, just in case he wanted to come home in the meantime.

Avery: I'm talking to Jack at 6 p.m. Do you mind if I do it from the living room? The internet connection is better.

Sam: I don't mind at all. Good luck! By the way, after that, you're mine for the rest of the evening.

Avery: ???

Sam: That's right. I promised to behave until today. Time's up.

I was completely giddy, and for a few seconds, I even forgot all about my nerves.

Avery: Okay. Game on.

I wanted to celebrate tonight, but I was afraid of making any plans until after I spoke to Jack. But he wouldn't have suggested a call if he didn't like what I sent him, right?

At ten to six, I paced the living room, trying to ignore the knot in my stomach.

At six on the dot, I clicked the Zoom link he sent me.

Jack was in his late fifties, possibly early sixties, with dark brown hair cropped short.

"Avery," he said curtly. His background was a sterile white office with a cactus in the corner.

"Hi, Jack. Nice to meet you."

"I've looked over your presentation."

Straight to the point—I could get used to it.

"Do you have questions?" I asked.

"No. Look, I didn't want to cancel this because we'd already set it up."

My stomach plummeted.

"I googled your previous company," he continued. "You've got a bad rep since you still haven't paid Austin Production what you owe them."

I took in a deep breath. That wasn't readily available information, but with a bit of digging, anyone could find it out. He might not be a man of pleasantries, but Jack did his homework, and I respected that.

"Jack, I'll be honest. I'm still working on paying that off. But in order to do it, I need to be able to sell more products. I don't want to make it sound like I'm blaming someone else, but my previous business partner embezzled funds."

"Then you have a legal case against them."

"I don't. I made a classic beginner mistake and didn't hire a second lawyer to go over our contract."

His face fell. I knew how that sounded. At best, I was making excuses. At worst, I was a moron. I couldn't deny it—I'd been exactly that. Too broke to seek out a lawyer and too excited that someone believed in my ideas.

"I take full responsibility, and I will pay them," I insisted. "I'm making monthly payments from my savings."

"I'll be honest. I don't want any part in that. Sounds like you could get into cash-flow issues."

"Jack, I—"

"I'm sorry, but it won't work out. After your issues with Austin Productions are gone, feel free to contact me again."

I swallowed hard. It could take years until I paid that off. And without another business up and running? It was impossible.

"Thank you for your time, Jack."

"I wish you the best of luck, Avery."

I stared at the screen for a long time after the call disconnected, giving in to tears. None of the other factories had replied to me. They probably all did their research and found the same thing.

I didn't even blame them. I just wasn't sure what to do next.

My phone beeped next to my laptop.

Mom: How did it go?

My heart broke. I didn't want to disappoint her. She'd gotten her hopes up even more than I had.

Avery: It didn't work out after all.

Mom: :(I'm sure it will soon.

Avery: I'm sure as well. Love you, Mom.

Mom: Love you more, baby girl.

I didn't want to worry her, but I wasn't sure this would work out at all anymore.

I called my sister, knowing she was waiting for my news as well.

"Hey, girl. That was a short call. How did it go?" she asked.

"He doesn't want to work with me. Did his due diligence and knows about my debt."

"Crap. That's frustrating."

"I'm not sure what to do now."

"Listen, you're talented, and your customers love you. Don't put any pressure on yourself. I'm sure you'll come up with something."

Her faith in me gave me energy. "Thanks, Jamie."

We chatted a bit about my jewelry, but she had a date tonight, so we said our goodbyes only a couple minutes later.

Biting the inside of my cheek, I texted Sam.

Avery: Call is already over. We're not going to work together.

Sam: Sorry about that! I'll be there soon.

To my surprise, he came in a few minutes later.

"What happened?" he asked, sitting down next to me.

"He's not confident in working together because I've yet to pay what's owed to our last manufacturer."

"You're still paying that? But it's not your fault."

I closed my laptop, pushing my chair back and rising to my feet. I needed to walk for a bit. I had too much adrenaline. I wasn't a runner, but in moments like this, I understood why people said they did it for stress relief.

"The contracts were in my name. That's why she cleaned out all the money."

"Declan can look over your contracts. He's good at that stuff and will find a loophole."

My heart swelled. "I suppose it wouldn't hurt. But I don't think he can do much. I was way too stupid when we drafted the contract and agreed that I couldn't sue her for taking out funds from the company."

"Avery, you're not stupid. You just let your heart get in the way."

"That shouldn't happen in business. But I'll figure something out. I'm just drawing a blank right now."

"I know you will." He looked at me intently. "I have full confidence in you. But it's also okay to admit that this just sucks."

"Of course it sucks, Sam. But if I allow myself to fall apart because of this, I don't think I'll get back up. It's been a few months now of hitting roadblocks." Which was true; I felt like I was taking one step forward only to take two steps back.

"Come on, let's go out."

"I forgot about that," I said, not totally in the mood to enjoy myself. I wasn't one for pity parties, but I could throw myself one tonight.

"I'll cheer you up, the way you did for me the other evening."

"Sam, you'd had a terrible day at the hospital and lost a lot of patients. People died. That's nothing compared to this."

"It's not fair to compare people's problems. Each of our struggles are unique to what we do. It doesn't mean they're any less important. " He stepped closer, pushing strands of hair from my chest and my shoulder. The gesture was strangely intimate and comforting. He looked me in the eyes. "What do you want to do?"

I cocked a brow. "You don't have a plan? The secret one you've been working on for a while?"

"I do, but I thought I'd ask just in case there was something specific you wanted to do."

"I trust you fully tonight," I told him. "Do with me whatever you want."

He grinned, and his blue eyes darkened a notch.

I pressed my lips together. "That was not an innuendo."

"I see."

"You do?" Because I was totally lost.

"Yes."

"Don't make me regret it."

"Not a chance."

* * *

Sam

"Where are we going?" She looked at me, moving her lips playfully from one corner to the other. Damn, I forgot she did that. She was cute.

"Do you still like ice skating?"

"With you? Hell yes." She clapped her hands once, shimmying her hips.

I wanted to push her against that wall and sink inside her. First I'd capture her mouth, then mark the rest of her body.

Shit, this is already escalating.

"I've reserved slots at Maggie Daley Park. Let's go."

"I don't have ice skates."

"We'll rent some."

"I need forty minutes to get dressed."

I stared at her. "Wait, you're... Are you serious?"

"Oh yeah."

"You look great. Let's go."

"I'm wearing sweatpants."

"You look hot." In fact, she was so damn gorgeous that it was hard to look away. The pants were a simple black fabric, but they were plastered to her, showcasing the curve of her ass. It was mouthwatering.

"Sam, I can't go out like this."

I growled. "Whatever. Go change."

She put her hands on her hips. "That was an awfully quick change of heart."

"You're right. No one should see you like this. No one but me."

"Sam."

"Yeah, I'm possessive and territorial, and there's nothing you can do about it."

She threw her head back, laughing. The sound was intoxicating. "So, if it were up to you, I'd wear a garbage bag and a coat tonight."

"Something like that. Or a tent."

She pointed at me, closing the distance and poking my chest.

"You, Sam, are going to find out that not everyone likes to play by your rules, and I the least of everyone."

"Let's take a break tonight from all our guidelines, okay?"

"Genius idea."

I was barely holding myself back from grabbing her wrist and pulling her even closer until my mouth was on hers. Instead, I exhaled sharply, watching her saunter through the loft, then up the stairs to her room.

I needed to be with her out in public so I wouldn't devour her. I wanted Avery more than anything else. I wanted to get to know her intimately again. I craved the closeness we'd had years ago.

Why the hell did I ever think we could just be roommates?

14

AVERY

*W*e arrived at the Skating Ribbon at Maggie Daley Park about forty minutes later. I was smiling from ear to ear, looking around. It was right in the city, surrounded by tall buildings. The rink snaked around the park in a twisty way. It was a trail, not a circular rink. If I remembered, some parts were uphill too. It would be a nice workout.

"Oh, I remember the Rink Cafe," I said.

It was a red food truck. Well, food truck wasn't the right term, as they mostly sold drinks. There were tables and benches in front of it, and quite a few people were sitting down, mostly teenagers but some adults too. I imagined that in the earlier hours, parents with young kids were also milling around.

We'd rented skates at the entrance in the park and were now walking awkwardly in them. At least I was. Sam seemed as confident as ever.

"When's the last time you skated?" I asked.

"With you."

My stomach squeezed. "I haven't been since then either," I admitted, adjusting my beanie. I'd put it on because I didn't want to risk my ears freezing off while I was skating. I loved that the rink was outdoors, though; we had a fantastic view of our surroundings.

"I thought this was like riding a bike, but I'm not quite so sure anymore," I said as we stepped onto the ice. My legs were a bit wobbly.

"Still trust me?" Sam asked.

"Yeah."

"I'll guide you at first, and then we'll see if you can do it on your own."

"Thanks."

He held out his hands and stood in front of me, grinning. Butterflies erupted in my stomach when I put my hands in his, even though we were both wearing gloves. He started moving backward, gliding effortlessly, pulling me with him.

"Hey, this isn't fair. You can skate backward, and I barely remember how to stand straight."

"It'll only take a few minutes," he said encouragingly, looking over his shoulder every now and again to make sure he wasn't bumping into anyone.

He was right; it was becoming easier by the second. I looked around, having forgotten how surreal it felt to skate between the skyscrapers. There were lots of speakers throughout the skating rink, playing all sorts of fun tunes.

After a few minutes, I told Sam, "You can let go now. I think I'm fine on my own."

He let go of one hand first and then the other.

"Yeah, I can do this," I exclaimed triumphantly, using my hands to keep my balance by moving them by my sides like I would do if I were jogging.

"I like skating this late in the evening," I said. We both had curfew at 8:00 p.m. back in high school, so we never came out this late. There were fewer people this time of night, and it was quite romantic under the moonlight. I liked feeling the breeze on my face. Sometimes I caught a whiff of Sam's cologne—and what do you know, my knees weakened exactly during those moments.

Coincidence, I was sure.

"You were right. This was just what I needed," I said as we skated side by side.

"I'm glad to hear that. You look more relaxed."

"I am. This week has been a tad insane, so I'm happy I get to cool down a bit. Thank you for bringing me out here."

"My pleasure."

We skated in silence for the next half hour. Getting more and more confident, I increased my pace.

"Hey, do you think I can still do a pirouette?" I asked Sam. We'd been out on the ice for two hours, and I knew we'd probably call it a night soon. I could try a revolution or rotation or whatever the heck they called it in artistic skating.

"Sure. Why not?" Sam said. "Got the doctor right here if you need one."

I laughed. "Thanks for the vote of confidence."

I stopped by the entrance. I bit my lip, stretching out my hands, one in front and one in the back, before simultaneously moving them sideways. Gathering momentum, I performed my pirouette.

For a brief moment, I thought I did it. Then I realized I was losing my balance. I wasn't sure where the moon or the ice was.

"Holy shit," I exclaimed. The ice was definitely coming closer to my face.

"I've got you," Sam said. He reached for me just as my ass hit the ice. My tailbone took the brunt of the impact. Thankfully he caught my head before I could hit that too.

"I've got you," he repeated.

"My instincts are shit. Why didn't I put my hands down first?"

"It's good you didn't. You might have broken a wrist. Think you can stand?"

I nodded. "Yes." My tailbone was still protesting, but it wasn't too bad.

He chuckled, looking at me.

"Why are you laughing?"

"You look cute with your beanie all lopsided." He came closer to me, straightening it up before running his hands through the hair hanging below it. "You're so damn beautiful."

"You aren't just a knight in shining armor anymore but one with an official diploma. The way you rushed to my side, putting your hand under my head? Pure sexiness gold."

"You saw that? You were in free fall."

I tapped my temple. "No, but I'm very good at imagining how things went."

We both started laughing, and then his lips were on mine. He moved them slowly, and I opened up without reservation. This evening was magic, and I wasn't going to fight it.

He deepened the kiss, groaning against my mouth. Even though it was cold outside and my tailbone was still sore, I got so turned on, I could've jumped him right there.

Someone cleared their throat.

"The ice rink is closing," a female voice said.

We flew apart like we'd been electrocuted. I lost my balance again, and Sam put a steadying hand on my back while the woman glared at us.

"We're heading out right now," I said, fighting a smile.

Out of the corner of my eye, I saw Sam doing the same.

We hurried to the rental kiosk. It was awkward to walk with quick steps in the skates, but who cared? After we returned them, we headed to the car. Sam drove home at top speed.

"Hey, that was a red light," I said.

"Was it?"

"Yeah."

"I didn't see."

"Sam, how could you not see?"

"Too busy imagining all the things I'll do to you when we get home."

I sucked in a breath, licking my lips. I fidgeted in my seat. "Make sure you get us home in one piece."

"Will do."

He parked in the inner courtyard of the building. We were both completely silent as we went upstairs. My breath heaved in and out. Too excited and caught up in him, I didn't question anything. I didn't want to.

The second we were inside the loft, his mouth was on mine. Oh yeah, this kiss was as deep, dirty, and wet as the one he gave me several days ago. I instantly soaked my panties. He groaned against my mouth as we took off each other's jackets. I didn't even remember when we got rid of our gloves.

He paused, cupping my face and wrapping his other hand in my hair. "Avery, are you sure?"

"Yes. Yes," I said. "God, yes."

He gave me a wicked smile. "Your room or mine?"

I grinned. "Yours." I hadn't seen his room since we moved in.

We kissed desperately on the way up, taking off our clothes. I heard something rip, probably my tights, but who cared?

When we entered his room, I noticed he also had a desk just like mine. He kissed me against it, making me tremble with every lash of his tongue. He moved his hands slowly over my body, but even so, they betrayed his deep and relentless hunger. He wanted me, and I wanted nothing more than to climb him right there and then. He was so damn sexy.

Taking a step back, he looked at me slowly from head to toe before coming right back in front of me. He slid one hand between my legs, pushing his thumb against one thigh and his pinkie against the other one.

"Spread wide for me, babe."

My knees buckled as I moved my feet wider apart. My center was pulsing like crazy with anticipation. I sucked in a breath, watching him tilt his mouth forward, capturing mine. When I felt the tip of his fingers on my clit, I broke out in a sweat, shuddering. I gave in to him completely, enjoying the unbelievably amazing sensations. He moved his tongue and fingers slowly, driving me crazy. Then I suddenly felt cold as he dipped his fingers lower. I groaned, putting my hands on his shoulders as my thighs weakened.

He slid two fingers up and down my entrance. Pleasure gripped my nerve endings. I was on fire.

I didn't think it could get better.

But then it did because he pushed two fingers inside me, making a come-here motion. I was lost in the sensations, moaning every time he brushed my clit with the heel of his palm, crying out when his fingers reached my G-spot.

I was done for. I climaxed so quickly and so damn hard that I was almost ashamed.

"Babe. You're amazing."

My legs shook. I'd never come so fast. Then again, I'd been on edge for weeks.

"I want you inside me," I said. "I'm clean. And on the pill."

"I'm healthy too." His eyes flashed as he hooked an arm around my waist, pulling me flat against him. My breasts were squished between us, the hard muscles of his torso grinding against my soft flesh.

Abruptly, he turned me around.

"Spread your legs," he murmured in my ear.

Sucking in a breath, I obliged. I felt his hand at the base of my spine, moving up slowly to the middle of my back and pushing lightly. I received the message and lowered myself onto the desk.

Oh God. I felt no shame at being sprawled out like this, completely naked.

I looked over my shoulder. My skin turned to goose bumps as I watched him arch over me, kissing my back. And then I felt one of his hands between my legs. He pressed three fingers against my heated flesh, moving them lazily up and down. My thighs shook, and my fingers curled, as did my toes. If I were in a bed, I'd sink my fingers deep into a pillow, but since this was a desk, I pressed them into the hard surface.

His cock pushed against my right ass cheek, hot and hard, and I nearly broke out of my skin.

"Please," I murmured. "I need you."

He put the tip of his cock on my clit, then circled it.

I whimpered at the contact. "Inside me. I need you inside me."

I felt him move and sucked in a breath, bracing myself. I was so turned on, so damn wet. I was ready for him.

He pushed inside me the next second, and there was nothing gentle about it. He rushed in all the way. I welcomed the feeling. I was so full and sated, yet desperate for him at the same time.

His chest pressing against my back, he interlaced the fingers of our left hands. His right hand was on my breast. I felt like I was part of him. He thrust inside me, fast and relentless. He completely owned me. Tremors of pleasure rolled through my body, starting deep inside me. I knew that when I eventually climaxed, I'd be completely overwhelmed.

"You feel so damn good," he murmured in my ear.

The sound of our bodies moving against each other filled the room. His grunts vibrated against my back, and my own moans filled the air. We were both lost in each other. I was burning from the inside out, feeling him stretch me on the inside while his hands found all my sweet spots one after the other. He kissed the side of my neck, feathering his fingers from my breast down to my thigh. He seemed to touch me everywhere at once, and I wasn't sure I could take it anymore. I needed my release. I needed to come or I was going to implode.

Sweat trickled between our bodies while we glided against each other even faster. I kept one hand firmly on the edge of the desk, pushing my ass back into him. We were both wild and unrestrained.

"I'm not going to last long," he said in my ear. "But I want to feel you come before that. Do you understand?"

I couldn't find my voice, so I nodded before realizing he couldn't see me.

"Sam, I'm going to—" My voice broke when he pushed two fingers straight over my clit in a slow, gentle motion. I felt my pussy heat up. I squeezed my eyes shut, crying out loud as I exploded. The wave of pleasure was never-ending. My whole body was engulfed in flames.

Through the haze, I felt him come too. I figured my ears probably weren't working right because I couldn't hear a damn thing, but I definitely felt it. It was glorious to know I'd brought him into this state of abandon.

I wasn't sure how I was standing anymore, even with the table for support. My muscles felt like liquid. I realized he was partly supporting me with one strong arm wedged between me and the desk.

He held me like that for a few minutes before we both headed downstairs to the bathroom to freshen up. I had no idea how we managed to trudge back up the stairs afterward. Once we were in his bed, I lay on my belly, putting a pillow under my head and looking at him sideways.

"How are you feeling?" he murmured in my ear. "Are you comfortable?"

"Comfortable? This is the best night of my life. My muscles are starting to ache," I said. "I wonder if it's from the skating or from the sexy time."

"Depends where the ache is," he said in a serious voice.

I lifted my head. "Hey, that's your doctor tone."

"What?" he asked, laughing.

"Yeah, I heard it at the ice rink, too, when you caught me, just before you turned on that super-sexy Maxwell charm."

He groaned. "The Sam charm."

"Huh?"

"Not the Maxwell charm. Don't put me in the same group as my brothers."

I shimmied my hips. "Are you jealous or something?"

"No," he answered quickly.

"Then I'll continue calling it the Maxwell charm. I think there's something in your DNA. Even though you"—I pointed at him, touching his chest—"are putting an original spin on it, of course."

He blinked. "An original spin."

"This was so amazing," I told him as I felt my eyelids flutter shut. "The ice skating, the sexy time, and the Maxwell charm."

"The Sam charm," I heard him say as if from a distance.

I smiled. "Sam charm," I agreed before I went out like a light.

15

AVERY

"Hmm, these sheets are so soft," I muttered, blinking my eyes open. They were definitely not my marked-down, pilled cotton ones. They were satin.

I pushed myself up into a sitting position.

Oh, I'm in Sam's bed. That's right. He has fancy sheets.

I looked around for the man himself, but he wasn't in bed, or in the room. *What time is it?* He didn't have an alarm clock, and my phone wasn't anywhere in sight. I'd dropped my phone somewhere in the living room last night, along with the rest of my clothes. I was going to have to do the walk of shame to my room naked. Then again, it wasn't a particularly long one, but still, my heart hammered in my chest.

Is Sam home at all? I wasn't sure how things between us would be this morning. Last night, we agreed on a time-out, but when had it expired? At midnight? This morning? Or after he gave me the best orgasms of my life?

I found the towel I'd used last evening after we showered next to the bed and put it around me.

I tiptoed out of the room, descended the staircase, and immediately saw Sam. He stood in front of the window, sipping coffee.

He was wearing shorts but nothing else. *What's he trying to do? Cause a traffic accident?* He had no business flaunting his unbelievably sexy body. And maybe I was a tad possessive as well.

It happened once and that's all. A onetime thing. Don't forget that, I told myself as I went straight toward him, but I stalled midway, realizing I hadn't even checked my appearance.

I went in the bathroom instead. Yup, I looked like hell: puffy eyes, completely messed-up hair. I needed to put myself together before I faced the music. I dropped the towel to the floor and hopped in the shower, where I quickly washed my hair and face.

Typically, after a late evening out, I liked to put slices of cucumbers on my eyes and a mask to hydrate my skin. But for that, I'd have to lie down for thirty minutes so they could do their work. And I'd have to sneak into the kitchen, and—

You're being so ridiculous, Avery, a voice in the back of my mind chastised. *It was a sexy night together between two consenting adults. That's it. Don't make it into something else.*

It was perfectly acceptable for me to want to look my best, even though I'd just had sex with my roommate.

I groaned as I got out of the shower. *What was I thinking? What if things between us get so awkward, I have to move out? Why didn't I think this through?*

Well, because this was Sam. He was always my kryptonite, and apparently sixteen years of no contact hadn't changed that.

I blow-dried my hair before putting on a fluffy pink robe, then headed into the living room, drawing in a deep breath. Sam was still at the window, only he wasn't holding his cup anymore, and he wasn't facing the street. Instead, he was looking straight at me.

My breath caught. He beckoned me forward with his right forefinger, and I instantly moved toward him as if he was pulling strings on a puppet.

"Good morning," he said when I was close enough.

"Hey." My voice sounded like a hiccup. *What is wrong with me?*

"You stayed so long in that bathroom, I thought you might try to escape."

"You saw me earlier?" I asked on a grin.

"Yeah, but before I had time to call out, you'd already run away."

"I needed to make myself presentable," I said.

"Avery, you look fucking sexy no matter what."

I licked my lips. *So much for a time-out.*

Sam continued. "I like seeing you unkempt because of me. Your hair wild because of me, because we had fantastic sex."

Oh. My. God. I glanced out the window, down to the street, anxious to change the course of this conversation before I combusted. "Why are there so many people awake at this hour? Don't they have anything better to do than stare at you?"

"What?" He chuckled.

My cheeks burned. "Never mind."

He stepped even closer, and I drew in a sharp breath. He smelled like his shower gel but no aftershave. In fact, up close, I could see that his five-o'clock shadow had turned into light whiskers. It felt delicious against my skin last night. I barely resisted the urge to reach out and see how they felt against my palm this morning.

I pointed at his torso. "Why do you have to stand in front of the window like that where everyone can see you?"

"Already marking your territory?" he asked, wiggling his eyebrows.

I swallowed hard, shaking my head. "Um, I know I'm indicating no, but I think the answer is actually yes. Don't ask me to explain it. I don't understand it myself."

We both started laughing. I felt even more self-conscious than before. I wrapped my robe tighter around me, which was completely unnecessary, just giving my hands something to do.

"Avery, I have a proposition for you."

My pulse sped up. "Oh?" I asked.

"Let's extend that break so it includes today."

"The whole day? Hell yes," I said, my smile stretching from one side of my face to the other.

He laughed. "I thought you'd fight me more on it."

"Do you want me to? I can totally start a fight. I just need a very strong coffee beforehand. I don't have a lot of energy. Someone worked me out really good last night."

His eyes darkened as he tilted toward me, and I stumbled backward. Without even turning around, he closed the drapes.

"What are you doing?"

"Not sure how long I can resist you. I want to cover my bases first. Wouldn't want anyone to peek inside."

"Sam Maxwell, are you intending to do shameless things to me in broad daylight?"

"Fuck yes." He came closer. "But I also want to just spend the day with you." He cupped my face, feathering the tip of his nose along my right cheek. "Last night was fun, but I want us to give ourselves a chance to relax around each other."

"Why?" My heartbeat accelerated.

He straightened up, looking me in the eyes. "It feels right." He frowned, pressing his thumb across the bow of my upper lip. "Anything against that?"

"No," I whispered.

"Pity, I was looking forward to convincing you." He focused on my mouth.

I congratulated myself for using my super-minty toothpaste. To my astonishment, he didn't kiss me.

"Let's get dressed and go out for breakfast and coffee. What do you think?"

"Mm." I put both my hands on his chest. "I kind of liked the dirty version of you."

"We have plenty of time for that too. I want to feed you first, and there's nothing in the fridge. The other day I saw a coffee shop that boasts the best pecan pie in the city. I double-checked the reviews, and they agree. It's still one of your favorites, right? If not, I'm sure they have something else."

I blinked, taking a step back. I was so stunned. I didn't know what surprised me the most, that he remembered my favorite or that he'd actually double-checked the reviews just to make sure he wasn't taking me to a crappy place.

"Yes, it is," I said.

He clapped his hands once. "Okay. Then let's meet back down here in twenty minutes," he said at the same time I said one hour. He growled, "Avery, I'm starving. I can't wait for an hour."

"Fine. I'll be quick."

"You've already showered."

"Yes, but I'd intended to style my hair and… Never mind. I'll be here in twenty minutes," I said. He was right. Why waste any second of our time-out day by getting ready? This was silly. I had one day where Sam was mine, and I wasn't going to waste a precious second of it.

I didn't manage to get ready in twenty minutes, though. It took me twenty-five. By the time I came downstairs from my room, I could tell Sam was already impatient. He was pacing the entrance area, and he'd put on his shoes. He was wearing jeans and a Henley shirt with a leather jacket.

It was a preppy look on him, but it was so damn sexy.

"What's with that smile?" he asked as I approached him.

"I was just thinking, 'Thank God you wear scrubs at work.' They hide some of that sexy body. Otherwise, you'd probably have patients clamoring over you."

"That still happens from time to time. I'm a hit, especially with women over sixty."

"Well, they have great taste, don't they?"

He offered me his arm, and I took it, pressing my ear briefly to his bicep.

"I love that we extended the time-out to today," I admitted.

He tensed up, and my stomach lurched. *Crap. Are we supposed to totally ignore the boundaries?* Straightening up, I didn't dare look at him.

Once out on the street, he extended his arm around my shoulders. It didn't matter what would happen tomorrow. I had today, and that was enough.

"First up is the pie, right?" I double-checked.

"Yeah."

I looked around, biting my lip. He brought his mouth to my ear. "They have excellent coffee. I looked at their machine too."

Goose bumps broke out on my skin. I'd always had a slight obsession with coffee machines in high school because I'd waitressed two afternoons a week.

I had no idea why the fact that he remembered those details about me meant so much. Did it mean he'd pined for me all these years? Or had the details resurfaced now that we'd seen each other? It didn't really matter.

We walked at a slow pace, soaking in the energy of our neighborhood. I truly enjoyed it. The streets weren't crowded, so it didn't even feel like Chicago. More like we were on vacation somewhere.

We arrived at the appropriately named The Coffee & Pie Shop a few minutes later. It was very cozy, with couches and armchairs spread around the room. They had an electric fireplace in the center. The way the flames danced could've fooled me into thinking it was real. It was early enough that there were still plenty of tables available.

"Sit down. I'll bring everything over," Sam said. I was getting a slice of pecan pie and coffee.

"You've got *fine* manners, Mr. Maxwell."

From behind, he touched both my shoulders, whispering in my ear, "Always. At least when we're out of bed."

A shudder went through me, and I shimmied in my seat. Maybe I should've asked for us to define *time-out* a little bit more.

Last night, I thought the break would include skating and a little flirting. And then we'd completely crossed the line.

But today, I was totally overthinking.

Breathe in and out, Avery.

It was a cold but sunny day.

"You look so relaxed," he said, startling me.

"That was fast. And with so many treats," I nearly screeched. He had brought not only pecan pie and coffee, but also cheese-cake with a strawberry topping and *mousse au chocolat*. "Oh, Sam. I think you're my favorite person right now."

"I like the sound of that." He winked, sitting down.

The three slices were enormous enough for both of us to share. And he hadn't lied about the coffee.

"This is good," I said. "Thank you for bringing me here."

"I love to please you, Avery."

I licked my lips, staring straight at him. "Okay, we need to define the parameters of this time-out."

"Go on." His eyes were scrutinizing me, making me squirm.

"Sexy talk is allowed?"

"Sure. Why wouldn't it be?"

"I don't know. How are we supposed to go back to being roommates after the day's over if we keep flirting with each other?" I answered in a whisper.

His eyes turned hard. "We'll figure it out." He sounded cold, or maybe he was determined.

"I don't want to spoil the day."

"You aren't. But I don't want us to worry about any of that right now."

"You're right," I said, taking a spoonful of the mousse. "You don't have plans with your family at all today?" I wanted to make sure, as I remembered him telling me that he used his time off between shifts to catch up with friends and family.

"I canceled everything I'd planned," he said with a straight face.

I gasped. "Because of me?"

"Hell yes."

"When did you do that?"

"This morning while I was waiting for you."

I leaned back in my chair, crossing my legs and tapping my top foot to a quick rhythm. "You were so sure I would say yes?"

"Avery." His voice was so rough that it startled me. My body reacted instantly as heat coursed through me. I pressed my thighs against each other to stop the sensation. "Last night was incredible. I figured I couldn't be the only one who didn't want it to end."

"Still," I said, trying to play it cool, "I don't like being considered a sure thing."

I'd only been teasing him, but his eyes turned intense.

"You'd never be a sure thing, Avery, no matter what. You've always been incredible. You *are* incredible. And I don't take anything that happens between us for granted. Not because we have history or because we're roommates. You deserve the very damn best of everything."

"Oh, another plus in the improvements column," I murmured. "You're so romantic."

"You're keeping tabs?" He curled his lips in a sly smile.

"Maybe."

"I meant every word."

"You brought me to a place with delicious pie, so clearly you practice what you preach."

"Always."

"Let's play a game," I suggested.

"I'm all ears."

"Let's ask each other questions, stuff we used to know about each other, and see what's still true and what's not."

"That's a great idea."

"I'll go first. Kimberly and Reese are still your best friends?"

"Sort of, but not like before. I spent too much time abroad. Although, Kimberly is about to move back home. She was away for a long time too. We're still very close, but it's much different than it used to be."

"Wait, where was Kimberly?" I'd been closer to her than to Reese, maybe due to the age gap.

"She's been living in Paris for the past few years. She's arriving next week. I'm thinking about taking her out to dinner. She loves discovering new restaurants, and I'm trying to figure out what she'd like. I need a way to find out without her catching on. If anyone in the family asks her, it'll be too obvious."

I pushed a strand of hair behind my right ear. "I can find out."

"How?"

"Just leave it to me. I'll message her on Facebook."

"Not sure she's got an account. I think I'm the only one in the family who does."

"How come?"

"Everyone deleted their accounts after the scandal with Reese's wedding."

I thought for a second. "I have an idea. Give me Kimberly's number. I'm going to catch up with her and pretend I want to ask her about Paris. It's always been my dream to go there. One thing will lead to another, and I'll find out exactly what you need."

He grinned. "You're resourceful."

"Yes, I am."

16

SAM

*A*very kept her promise. She spoke to Kimberly and found out her new favorite restaurant in Chicago was an all-American steak house on Pierce Avenue.

Reese and I arrived at the same time. She whistled appreciatively, looking at the entrance. The place was elegant, with tinted windows and an all-wood interior.

"How do you know this is her favorite now?" Reese asked.

"Avery spoke to her."

She winked. "You and Avery are getting close and cozy, huh?"

"Yes," I admitted.

"You'll have to elaborate on that."

"I don't see why," I jabbed.

She pushed my shoulder. "You're being mean."

"Nah, just teasing you. Did you come from the hotel?"

"Yes, but I spent the past hour at The Happy Place with Gran."

I was more than happy that they'd kept the bookstore running even after opening the hotel.

"Being there always takes me back in time," Reese said.

"I know. Me too."

"And Gran gives the best advice, I swear. Even when it comes to dating."

"You're seeing someone?" I asked a bit sharply.

"Ha! Think you can withhold information from me but can expect me to share everything?"

I cleared my throat. "No, I'm just surprised no one said anything."

Reese burst out laughing. "I was just making fun of you. I'm not currently dating anyone. Hopefully I'll go on a date soon—you know, sometime this century."

My cousin deserved all the happiness in the world. She was one of the kindest people I knew. But dating didn't come easy for her after the ordeal she went through with her ex-fiancé. Then again, if I found out my best friend slept with my partner, I'd probably give up on relationships altogether.

"Look, Kimberly is coming," I said, noticing her in the tinted window.

We turned around, waving at Kimberly as she got out of an Uber. My cousin definitely looked different since having moved to Paris, though I couldn't exactly say why. *Has she colored her hair? Or cut it?* I was clueless about these things.

"It's good to be back," she said when she was within earshot.

Reese and I each took one of her hands, pulling her closer. Reese kissed her left cheek and I her right.

Kimberly turned around, cocking a brow at me as we stepped inside.

"By the way, very smooth putting Avery on it. I deduced from our phone call that you're sleeping with her."

My jaw dropped.

Reese straightened with a jump. "Wait, how did you deduce that?" Turning to me, she added, "And is it true?"

I glowered at Kimberly. "Did Avery tell you that?"

"Oh my God, you're confirming it," she said.

Reese just exhaled sharply. Clearly she was at loss for words.

As we approached the host, he greeted us. "Welcome. Do you have a reservation?"

"Yes," I said. "Maxwell, for three."

"Right this way." He led us inside to a table by the window.

The place was too crowded and too loud for my taste, though it was better when we reached our table. With a window on one side, we only had the cacophony of voices hitting us from the other side. At least we weren't surrounded by it.

As we all sat down, I caught Kimberly grinning.

"What?" I asked.

"I like that we're already bickering before we even manage to order. This is like old times, isn't it? It's like no time has passed at all."

"Except it has," Reese said, opening the menu. "You've both been gone for far too long, and I'm still not used to having you back."

"Now, Sam, care to bring us up-to-date?" Kimberly asked.

"Jesus, cousin, let's order first, what do you think?"

"I already know what I want," she said. "The steak with sweet potato fries."

As the waiter approached us, I decided I wanted the same. In the end, all three of us ordered the steak but I didn't want the sweet potato fries, so I got regular ones with shredded cheese on top.

After the waiter left, Kimberly crossed her legs and then laced her fingers over one knee. "So?"

"Oh come on," I complained.

"What? For so long I only caught up with all of you via phone or video chats. Now it's the first time I get to gossip in person, and let me tell you, it feels wonderful."

Reese was still suspiciously silent.

"Should I worry about you not saying anything?" I asked her.

She bit her lip. "Well, I just don't know if it's a good idea, you sleeping with Avery."

"And why not?" I asked.

"You do have history, and things can become muddled. You didn't break up with your previous girlfriend too long ago. What if you're still on the rebound?"

"First of all, I didn't break up with her. She cheated. That has a tendency to kill everyone's affection. You should know that."

She winced.

I hung my head. "Fuck, I'm sorry."

"It's okay. And you do have a point. Our situations are similar, and it's because of that that I'm telling you this. Even when the other person wronged you, if you really were in love, it's not easy to erase them from your heart."

"Please tell me you're not still hung up on that moron?" Kimberly asked, voicing exactly what I was thinking.

"Not anymore," Reese replied. "I wasn't exactly hung up on him, but for so long, I kept wondering what she has that I don't. Why would he even need another woman? And my best friend, no less. I had some regrets that things didn't work out. Don't you feel the same?" she asked me.

"Actually, no. I'm glad I found out who she really was before things got even more serious." But talking to Reese got me thinking. What did that say about my relationship with Olivia? That it hadn't been as deep as I thought? Come to think of it, after Avery and I broke up, I couldn't stop thinking about her for years. I'd always chalked it up to the fact that I'd been young, and she'd been my first big love, but what if it ran deeper?

"Sam," Kimberly said, "not to be a party pooper, but I sort of agree with Reese. Unless, of course, you plan to get back together with Avery."

I shook my head. "Neither of us is planning that."

"Oh good. Because very bad things seem to happen to you when you make plans." Frowning, she added, "In fact, sometimes I feel like planning has the opposite effect. I don't know if it directly leads to self-sabotage, but things end up not happening anymore."

Reese and I exchanged a glance. "What are we talking about here, exactly?" Reese asked.

"Yeah, I'm not following," I admitted.

Kimberly shrugged. "My former boss wasn't who I thought he was."

"You told Travis you're not being appreciated there."

"Yeah, it was more than that. At one point he seemed to be into me. We were involved for a while."

Reese gasped. "Why didn't you tell me?"

Kimberly pointed at her. "Because I knew you'd look at me with that judgey expression."

"That's not what I'm doing. This is just my shell-shocked face," Reese said. "Okay, fine. I'm judging a bit. You know how things can turn out when you're sleeping with the boss."

"I thought things were good. We weren't super serious, but I thought it was going somewhere. Then he went on a vacation last year. And came back married."

I instantly saw red. "What the fuck?"

"What? How long was he on vacation?" Reese asked.

"One month. Apparently he found 'the one' and couldn't wait to even tell me things were over before marrying her. I obviously realized something was awry because he'd stopped texting me. But some people are like that. Out of sight, out of mind. Things were weird at the office afterward."

"I bet," I agreed.

"That sounds like a nightmare," Reese said.

"After a while, he left, and I had a new boss, but things simply lost their appeal for me," Kimberly explained. "Before, I was excited to live in Paris, and I was enjoying my French life, and then suddenly I just wasn't. And when I no longer enjoy something, I take a step back and reevaluate."

"I always liked that about you, Kim," I said. I was, as far as I knew, the only person who called her that. My whole family made fun of me. Apparently, I couldn't say her whole name as a toddler, and the shortened version just stuck.

"I'm happy to be home and working with Reese and Travis. I'm glad the three of us are working together. It feels good to build something of our own."

"I feel the same," Reese said.

I always felt left out in conversations like these. Tyler was the only one who shared this sentiment because he'd also chosen to do something that was completely unrelated to the family businesses. I was always on the outskirts unless someone was a patient at the hospital.

We received our food shortly after, and all three of us dug in.

"This place is a great find," I said. The steak was probably one of the best I'd had.

"Yeah, it's a great mix between American comfort food and some French accents. If there's one thing I do miss from France, it's the food. And being so close to London and our sister."

Growing up, their father, my uncle, wasn't around them much. He'd taken my aunt's death very hard and was distant for years. After he moved to London, they had even less contact with him. It was a shock to Gran and everyone else that Uncle Harvey had recently gotten married and had a daughter without telling anyone. Still, Reese and Kimberly had taken it in stride. My cousins were strong women.

I was happy Kimberly was back and that I was here too. Luke had always been the closest to our cousins, and I knew he was also happier now that she was back home. Obviously everyone was grown now, so protecting them didn't work the same way it had when we were kids. But just knowing we could meet up at any time and that I could warn in person any asshole not to mess with them was giving me some peace of mind.

"Say, about Avery," Kimberly said suddenly. "She seems different than when we were in high school."

"We're all grown-ups, Kim," I replied.

"How is it, living with her?"

"Fucking torture," I admitted.

Reese started laughing, and Kim followed her lead a few seconds later. They weren't giggles either; they were loud, unrestrained laughs.

"Oh my God," Reese said between breathing in and out. "I was waiting for you to fess up about that ever since the guys helped you move in."

"Really? How come?"

"Travis snatched a picture of you when you weren't looking. You looked very possessive. Like you were secretly thinking, 'Mine. *Mine.*'"

"You're insane," I said.

"Yes, but I also have a sixth sense."

"I think you're treading in dangerous territory just by living together," Kimberly said.

"Why are you so adamant about not getting back together?" Reese added.

"Doesn't seem to be what she wants," I replied carefully.

During our time-out, she'd repeatedly brought up what would happen afterward. She'd set the boundary, and I was respecting it, even though I was walking around with a fucking hard-on every time I was at home. This wasn't just about sexual attraction though. Avery and I had a deep bond once, and living with her now had only reminded me of how strong it had been.

"Oh, but you want it," Kimberly said, correctly interpreting my expression.

Reese laughed. "The more things change, the more they stay the same, don't they?"

I shook my head, smiling to myself. They were both right. And it was high time I proved it to Avery.

17

AVERY

*D*espite loving the loft, I was getting cabin fever. The thought of staying in all day, every day, slowly started to stress me out. I liked having my private space and alone time, but I missed interacting with people, even just a little bit.

I researched coworking locations around the city, but most of them wanted some sort of agreement, either monthly or weekly. That wasn't what I was looking for. I wanted something flexible where I would wake up every morning and see if I wanted to go in or not. In the end, it seemed coffee shops were still my best option.

I invested in a pair of great noise-canceling earphones to take with me in case things got too loud. I liked people, but I didn't like the noise. It interrupted my creative flow.

I went to a coffee shop two blocks away from Alana's gallery. She promised to drop by after work. The second I stepped inside, I knew this place would ignite my creative juices. They had long tables made out of wood with benches on one side, but those looked a bit uncomfortable. On the other side, they had armchairs and low coffee tables. I opted to sit there. I could hold my sketch pad on my legs, and when I started working on administrative tasks, I could do the same with my laptop.

I ordered a coffee with skim milk and a bagel for breakfast. There were a few others here already. I couldn't tell if they were creative types or not, though no one was wearing a suit.

I was already feeling much more energetic than at the loft. On the plus side, it wasn't loud, since it wasn't too crowded yet. I did my best creative work in the morning, so my plan was to start with a few sketches for my upcoming collection.

I'd woken up yesterday with a completely new vision, and I was excited to start working on it.

Since I couldn't secure a contract with a factory, I could offer handmade jewelry. This, of course, was another business model altogether, so I was going back to the drawing board. But I was excited. We'd had craft courses for jewelry in college, so I knew the nuts and bolts, but I still had a lot to learn.

I had a good feeling about doing everything by myself. It meant I was in charge. If I could perform every part of my business, then I wasn't depending on anyone.

As I took out my sketch pad, my phone beeped with a message.

Sam: Hey, I just woke up, and you're not home. Where did you go?

One of the reasons I felt uncomfortable in the loft this past week was because I didn't know how to be around Sam. Granted, our schedules still didn't intersect much, but on the few mornings we'd both been home, things had been awkward. I figured it would be easier if I wasn't in the way. On the days when he had a shift, he was normally out of the house before I woke up and came back when I was already asleep.

I texted him back quickly.

Avery: I wanted a change of scenery, so I came to Kuzco Coffee Shop. It's great.

I snapped a picture, sending it to him.

Now, why had I done that? He hadn't asked for it.

Sam: That looks good. Are you going to spend the whole day there?

Avery: That's the plan. Fingers crossed, I get to be creative.

Sam: Fingers crossed.

I waited a few seconds more, curious if he'd say anything else, but he didn't. I felt awfully disappointed, but I'd come here with a goal, which was five sketches. I worked best in sprints, so I put the phone on the table in front of me and started the countdown while I began working on the first piece.

As usual, when I had the sketch pad in one hand and a pencil in the other one, the line simply flowed. I never knew where my inspiration came from. I figured it was a combination of all the things I saw and experienced in my day-to-day life. I liked to first sketch everything with a simple pencil so I wouldn't interrupt my flow by searching for colors. If I was happy with a sketch in black-and-white, I would redo it in color. I took a layered approach to everything. It was as if my mind couldn't come up with all the details at the same time.

Thankfully, no one interrupted me by calling or messaging. Alana and Sam were the only people I texted with regularity, and they both knew I didn't like to receive messages in the morning.

Before long, I lost myself in my sketches, as usual. After lunch, I worked on six orders I got on Fiverr for logo designs.

I snacked a lot during the day, mostly because I was there, and it was available. I ate one more bagel, the most delicious grilled cheese, pancakes, and even a muffin. *Ugh.* I'd have to stop that if I continued to use this place as my office; otherwise, I'd definitely put on unwanted weight with all the extra carbs.

"Hello, stranger," Alana exclaimed, making me wince.

I glanced at the clock before closing my laptop.

"Holy shit. It's already past six," I said.

"Oh yeah. The second I saw 5:59 p.m., I ducked out of the gallery. Not that anyone came in for the past hour, but I have to stay there anyway."

I surged to my feet, kissing her cheek before we both sat down. She looked at the table.

"You ate well today. I thought I'd find you here, starving."

"Oh, not at all." I pointed at the plate with a muffin. "This isn't all I had, by the way."

"You said you never remember to order food once you get engrossed in work."

I frowned. "Wait a second. I didn't order anything."

I startled in my chair, rewinding the day. Was I suffering from temporary memory loss? Had I been so lost in my sketches, Fiverr orders, and then research that I didn't remember ordering? But that was impossible, because I had a clear image of me placing an order this morning. Why would I not remember the rest?

As the waiter came to take Alana's order, he looked at me. "Miss, is there anything else I can get you?" he asked me after Alana ordered a decaf cappuccino with almond milk.

"I know this might sound weird, but did I order everything I got today?"

"No." He didn't even miss a beat.

My eyes bulged. "Okaaay, so you have a policy of serving customers who don't order stuff? Not that I'm complaining because I've loved everything, but how could you tell I needed food and what to give me?"

"We got a call this morning from a guy, name was Maxwell something."

"Sam," I whispered.

"That's right. Exactly. He opened the tab and gave us his credit card information. Told us you like bagels and cheese and coffee with skim milk and to bring something to snack on every couple hours or you were going to starve."

My jaw dropped. Alana was snickering.

"Thank you," I said.

Well, at least I wasn't going crazy.

"Do you need anything else?" he asked.

"I'm pretty full from all the snacks. Some water, please?"

"Right away, ma'am."

After he left, Alana pinned me with her gaze. "Your sexy roommate is clearly trying to woo you."

"He is?" I asked.

Alana frowned. "Girlfriend, what do you think this is called? How did he even know you're here?"

"I told him, and then I didn't hear from him again."

"He probably knew you'd have his balls if he interrupted you while you were in your creative mode."

I was still reeling that Sam had actually called here to make sure I wasn't starving.

"Oh shoot, I should thank him." I took out my phone, immediately typing.

Avery: Sam, I just found out you spoke with the coffee shop this morning. Thank you so much. Everything was delicious.

He answered a few minutes later.

Sam: You're welcome. Are you on your break?

Avery: Yeah.

He called me the next second. I shimmied in my seat, blushing.

"Go on, take that," Alana said in a playful tone.

I raised my hand at her, shaking my head. But she was right. I couldn't just ignore it. It would be rude.

I answered, sinking into my armchair.

"Hey, I'm glad you liked everything."

"I did. They brought some of my favorite things."

"I asked them to read me the menu, and I pointed out stuff I knew you'd like."

"Oh, Sam." I was stunned.

"Couldn't let you starve, could I? Actually, I think it's a great idea that you're working at coffee shops. I can't get anyone to feed you at home when I'm not there. It's easier when you're someplace that serves food, and the staff there was more than willing."

"You can't open a tab everywhere."

"Yes, I can." *Holy shit, he sounds serious.* "How was your day?"

"It was very productive. Now I'm ready to catch up with Alana."

"She's there right now?"

"Yes," I said.

"Then I can't break out the bedroom talk."

I gasped. I was sure my cheeks were so red, you could see them from the moon.

"Sam," I whispered.

"Are you blushing?"

"I think I am."

"So that means she knows what I'm saying anyway."

Alana was looking at me with a smug smile.

"I'm going to the bathroom," she said loud enough for Sam to hear.

"And now she's giving us space. I've always liked her," he said.

I licked my lips. "Why would you want to talk dirty now anyway?"

"Because I know how it affects you. I like knowing you're blushing for me. That you're somewhere in this city, and just because you're with me on the phone, your pulse quickens and you're wet."

I gasped again. "Can anyone hear you?"

"No, I'm alone in the doctors' lounge. I don't know why no one comes here."

I bit my lower lip. "Sam, what are you doing? I mean, the time-out is over."

"I know."

"Is this your way of asking for another one?" I tentatively started to feel optimistic.

"No."

"Oh." I felt completely disappointed.

"I don't want just a time-out, Avery. This past week, it's become obvious to me how much I want you. How much I need you in my life."

"Oh my God."

"But a time-out? We're not teenagers. I want you to be part of my life."

I swallowed hard. "I don't know what to say."

"You don't have to answer right now."

"You've prepped me for this," I said. I was in awe. "You kept me fed and well-caffeinated."

"Had to make sure you were in a great mood," he agreed. "I think it's working. You're not completely fighting me on this."

"I'm too stunned. And I still don't know what to say."

"Nothing. Absolutely nothing. I shouldn't have said anything anyway. This wasn't the plan."

Sam was too cute. He had a plan. "What do you mean?"

He cleared his throat. "Never mind." *This day is getting better and better.* "We'll talk at home."

"Okay. Alana's coming back anyway."

"Give her my best."

"I will."

I pocketed my phone just as Alana sat down in front of me.

She grinned. "I'm assuming your 'No way am I falling in love with Sam Maxwell' is soon going to turn to 'Yes way'?"

"I'm not sure of anything right now. He said all the right things."

"So what's the problem?"

"I don't know. I'm afraid of falling back in love with Sam. It could be amazing, or it could be devastating."

Alana frowned. "The uncertainty is the fun part. And let's face it. You went out with enough guys who just said the wrong things. Why not go out with the one who says the right things?"

18

AVERY

*O*nce I got home, I looked around. My heart was beating insanely fast. *Is Sam already here? He said he'd meet me.*

"Sam?" I called, but I got no answer.

A huge bouquet of flowers on the kitchen island caught my attention. He got my favorites—peonies. I practically ran toward the island, burying my nose in them and drawing in a deep breath. I couldn't believe he remembered these were my favorite flowers, or that he found them at this time of year. They weren't exactly in season.

I was so busy smelling them that I didn't notice he'd left a card for me. I looked at it greedily: **Do you want to go out with me? If yes, then turn the card around.**

I grinned, doing just that.

Come upstairs on the roof. Wear warm clothes.

Oh my God. He was waiting for me on the roof. I didn't even know we could use it.

I licked my lips, glancing at the card and the flowers and trying to judge if I would freeze my ass off if I went on the roof the way I was dressed. Yeah, I probably would. I was wearing a very thin sweater and a skirt with sheer tights, which had been fine for working indoors, but it wouldn't do for outside.

I ran toward my room, changing the sheer tights for wool ones. I also took off my oversized sweater and put on a nice top. It was definitely more of a summer outfit, but I paired it with an elegant sweater. I liked layering clothes in winter. Hurrying back to the living room, I put on my coat and a beanie.

I was giddy as I stepped out of the loft and headed up the fire escape. My heart seemed to thump harder with every step I took on the metal staircase, wondering what Sam was doing up here. Maybe we were just going to stargaze or something for a bit and then go back down. Although, he probably wouldn't have told me to dress in warm clothes if that was the case.

When I reached the rooftop, my jaw dropped. He'd arranged an outdoor date, complete with a firepit. "Oh my God, Sam. I can't believe this. A firepit?"

"I know you love it," he said. "And I charmed you that way once, so I thought it might work again."

I was instantly transported to that night. It was in our senior year of high school. We went for a weekend in the mountains with our whole class. Our cabin had a fireplace, too, and when the others went out skiing, I pretended to be sick, and Sam pretended not to want to ski. We were seniors and good students, so our teachers felt confident leaving us alone. They shouldn't have because we did what teenagers do and got down and dirty right in front of the fire.

I grinned at him. "It definitely worked, yes."

He smiled brilliantly, even taking out his phone and playing romantic jazz music. My heart was so full that I was barely keeping myself in check. I felt the need to dance and jump him and kiss him all at once.

"Where did you get the firepit? And how are we even allowed here?"

"The firepit was easy. They're for sale everywhere, especially at this time of the year. And you're right, we're not allowed on the roof, but the owner was easily swayed."

I gaped at him. "Easily?"

"I have to say my charm works in unexpected ways."

"Do I want to know? I don't think so."

As I came closer to him, I realized he must have actually brought furniture up here. "Sam, when did you plan all this?"

"I work fast, and I have a lot of Maxwells who jumped at the opportunity to help me."

"Who exactly?"

"Travis gave me the outdoor furniture from the hotel. Kimberly asked me to send her a picture of my firepit and then immediately decided this place needed more romance, so she came over with some blankets. I don't know what she did, but the place definitely looks better since she worked her magic."

I noticed a thermos next to the firepit. "What's in that?" I asked.

"Mulled wine."

There was also a pizza box.

"Oh, we're having dinner here," I said.

"Yeah, babe, we are." He held out a hand for me, and I took it with a bit of trepidation. He squeezed my fingers, pulling me close. "Thank you for accepting my invitation to the date."

"You made a convincing case," I whispered.

It smelled so good, like winter and fire and a hint of his cologne that still remained, though it was very subtle.

"I've been thinking about how to do this for some time now."

"You have?" I murmured.

"Yes."

My nerves got the better of me. I bit my lip, shivering.

"Talk to me, Avery. I know something's holding you back, but I don't know what."

"It's just that… you're freshly out of a relationship."

He blinked, pulling back, looking absolutely stunned. "Right. Yeah."

"And you moved here for her."

"I'm not following."

"I don't want to be your rebound, Sam."

His eyes widened. He leaned into me again, putting a hand on the side of my face and sliding two fingers under my beanie. "Avery, that couldn't be further from the truth. In fact, the opposite is true. Since meeting you again, I realized everyone since you has been a rebound."

My breath caught. "Sam, do you mean it?"

"Yes. Fuck yes, I mean it."

He kissed me, gently and hungrily at the same time, biting my lower lip lightly. I moaned against his mouth, melting in his arms. I was suddenly so warm that I felt the need to take off my coat, maybe even my clothes and underwear if the night continued this way.

He groaned, pulling back. "Come on, let's enjoy this fire and our food."

We sat down on the pillows, and I realized the blankets were actually a good idea because I suddenly felt chilled without Sam warming me up. He took the thermos, pouring mulled wine in two cups. I grabbed the pizza box, opening it and grinning at him.

"This is the best date ever."

"Fuck, you're cute."

I looked up at him and was surprised at the warmth in his eyes.

"What?" I asked.

"I like seeing you happy."

My stomach somersaulted. I took a huge bite of pizza. I wasn't hungry, but I wanted to enjoy everything about this evening—the man, the food, the wine, and the fire. I loved that we had a fire. It warmed me up on the inside that he'd wanted to recreate that evening from our past. He'd gotten the details right. We'd ordered pizza that night, too, although this one was a lot better. And we snuck some mulled wine over from the main cabin. Minors weren't allowed to drink, of course, but Sam had been very convincing even back then. Since neither of us was of drinking age, we'd gotten tipsy pretty fast. I was sure that wouldn't be the case this time.

"I can't believe this needed the Maxwell team effort."

"Hey, I had the idea, just not the skills to execute it. And I needed everything to be perfect for you."

* * *

Sam

I WAS proud of this evening. My family was going to tease me about getting their help for a long time to come. But one thing I learned during my work in Doctors Without Borders was that group efforts were almost always better than doing it all alone, and I needed everything to be perfect. I wanted this woman.

Fuck, how I wanted her.

I knew this with utmost certainty, even though so many other things in our lives were up in the air.

We ate the pizza quickly but took our time with the mulled wine. Avery shivered a bit.

"Want me to find another blanket?" I asked.

"No, but I wouldn't mind some body heat." She wiggled her eyebrows.

"Hey, I'm trying to be romantic here, not maul you before you've even finished your wine."

"Maul away, Maxwell. I don't mind."

I undid my jacket, and she did the same. She had a sweater underneath. I moved closer until our sides were touching, then placed my arm around her shoulders to keep her warm. The rooftop was encircled by tall glass panels, so it was windproof, but I didn't want to risk her being uncomfortable.

She looked at the fire and sighed. And then I realized she had one hand under my shirt.

I grinned. "Avery."

"Yes?" she murmured.

"Behave."

"I don't think so."

Well, fuck me. I instantly turned hard.

Tipping her head up, I kissed her, then completely forgot that I'd planned for us to stay on the rooftop the whole evening. I couldn't think past how much I wanted to explore her body.

And when she moaned against my mouth, tugging at my shirt, I knew she was right there with me.

19

SAM

I got us both up on our feet, calculating the fastest way to get downstairs. I found a good solution just as I turned off the propane and the fire died out. I put an arm under her knees and lifted her up. She smiled against my mouth as I carried her down the stairs.

Once we were inside the loft, I took off her beanie, jacket, and sweater. She took care of her boots.

"Wait a second," she murmured, stepping back in the dark. She reached under her skirt. I was about to ask what she was doing when she started yanking down her tights. Oh yeah. Easier access. I approved. Good thing she took care of those by herself; I probably would've ripped them apart.

Last time we were together, we'd been desperate for each other. There was desperation now, too, but it was different. That night, I knew I'd only have her for a limited time. But right now, I could take my time with her to make her come six ways from Sunday.

"I'm going to take off all your clothes slowly," I said.

"And then?" she asked, breathless.

"And then we'll see." I grabbed the hem of her top and pulled it over her head. She was wearing a bra that seemed to be the color of her skin. It was barely covering her nipples.

I took it off quickly. She was so damn gorgeous, her breasts peeking up at me. I licked my lips, putting one knee on the couch and bending so I was level with her right breast. I grabbed her ass beneath her skirt, pulling her closer to me while I wrapped my mouth around her nipple. I felt her body surge. She pressed her stomach into me.

"Oh, Sam."

Knowing I didn't have to hurry up to get my fill of her intensified every sensation. When I moved to the other breast, she wrapped her hand in my hair, tugging. My girl was getting wild. She needed me, but I was in no rush. I kissed down between her breasts to her navel as I yanked down her skirt. Then I rose, taking a good look at her panties. They were white and insanely sexy against her tan skin.

"Spread your legs wider," I said.

Her pussy was right in front of me. I rubbed my thumb over her panties from her clit down to her entrance, the fabric turning damp at my touch. Then I pulled it to one side, and before she realized what I was about to do, I leaned forward, licking her.

"Oh my God." Her voice shook. She clamped her hands on my shoulders, trembling.

I patted the couch right next to my thigh, "Put your right foot here."

She exhaled sharply, lifting a leg, just as I told her to. I was too greedy for her to take off her panties, so I just kept them to one side and covered her clit with my lips.

"Oh, Sam, Sam," she chanted, rocking her hips back and forth as I moved away from her clit, pressing the flat of my tongue against her heated flesh.

"You taste so good, babe." I slid a finger inside her, making a come-here motion, and she gasped, rolling forward. The leg she stood on bent.

I showed her no mercy. I nipped and licked at her clit, then alternated, pushing my finger inside. With the strokes of my tongue, I brought her closer to the edge.

"Sam. Please, Sam. Oh."

I took my mouth away from her just a fraction of an inch, but I spoke so that each word, each breath landed on her sensitive flesh.

"Do you want me to let you come?"

"Yes, please."

I was going to make her come once before I sank inside her. I clamped my lips again around her clit and sucked it into my mouth. She came undone the next second, and did so beautifully. The pleasure seemed to overwhelm her whole body, her back arching as her hips pushed forward. She took away the leg she'd put on the couch and then pressed her thighs together. She hunched her back and straightened up again.

"Oh my God," she murmured.

I instantly rose to my feet, putting both hands on her arms.

"Are you okay?"

"Hmmmm. Satisfied." Her eyes were closed. She was humming to herself. "Oh God, this was so unexpected and fast, and so damn good." She opened her eyes.

"And I'm not nearly done."

"I'm not sure if that's a promise or a warning."

"Both."

"Where do you want me?" she asked.

"Right here. At least for the first round."

Her eyes widened. "You have more plans?"

"Yes."

Taking a step back, she checked me out from head to toe before coming closer. She yanked at my shirt, pulling it over my head, and then she moved to my jeans, undoing the button and pulling them down. "You're ready for me."

"I've been ready since I got you naked, babe."

"You have excellent self-restraint." She wrapped her hand around my cock, squeezing it once, then took her hand away. "I just want you inside me."

"Not so fast," I murmured. "You're mine. I intend to enjoy it." I kissed her collarbone, speaking against her skin. "You're mine to explore, and not just tonight." I pushed her to sit on the couch and then raised her legs horizontally so she was on her back. I hooked my elbow under her ankles, lifting them, and kissed down her leg, dipping my tongue behind her knee. She rolled her hips back and forth, her telltale sign that this was a sweet spot for her. I kissed back up until I reached her ankle, then moved to the other leg. She was getting desperate again. I knew it by the way she tugged at the leather couch with her fingers. Then she grabbed both her breasts. I was going to remember the sight of her, driven to touch herself by sheer desperation, for as long as I lived.

I couldn't keep this up for much longer. I wanted to feel her flesh around me. Kissing up her torso, I moved to her arm, nipping it lightly.

I traced the side of her body with my fingers. I was so damn turned on that I was going to lose my mind soon, yet I hadn't had enough of her, not nearly enough. I explored her belly, alternating between a kiss and a bite before moving down her legs again.

"Oh, Sam."

I knew she needed more than this, a bit of relief. So while I kissed back up, I pressed my fingers around her, straight onto her clit.

"Sam." She was grinding against the backrest. "Oh God, Sam, I'm going to—"

"I know you are, babe, but when you come, I'll be inside you."

I kept moving my hand, feeling her entire body tighten up. I could tell she was getting closer by the way her breath hitched on every inhale and how she begged, saying my name over and over.

When she was just at the edge, I slid inside her. I was so turned on that I couldn't do it inch by inch, but she was so wet that it didn't matter. She let out a loud, animalistic groan when I was fully seated.

She hadn't come, not yet, but I knew she wasn't too far off. I didn't want to crush her. I sustained my weight by digging my knees into the couch and pushing a forearm against the backrest.

"Oh God, Sam." Her face was flushed.

"You're so damn beautiful," I said.

I started moving faster, thrusting harder, until I felt her spasm around me. Her orgasm was building up again, and she was pulling me with her. Feeling her flesh-on-flesh was out of this world. She was nearing the edge. This was torture for her. Her face was scrunched up with both pleasure and torment.

"Please… please," she murmured.

"I'm going to make you come, babe. Don't worry."

I only had to press my fingers lightly on her pussy for her to explode. She tightened around me so damn fast that my vision turned black for a few seconds. My mind spun. I shut my eyes tightly, thrusting even harder.

As she came back to her senses, I lost all of mine. A grunt tore from my chest. I felt it in my entire rib cage. My climax radiated in every corner of my body, completely taking me over. I lowered myself until my front was covering her chest, but because I slid slightly to one side, I wasn't crushing her.

"You're glorious," I said.

Her hair was sticking to her face. She tried with one hand to push it away but somehow only seemed to make more of a mess of it.

I kissed her shoulder lazily.

"Don't kiss me. I'm sweaty," she said.

"I like the taste of you. It's salty."

"You more than kept your promise," she murmured, "and now I think I'm going to fall asleep right here. How did I get so tired?"

"I'll carry you to bed."

She opened her eyes wide. "Really? Wow, that gave me a boost of energy. You can still carry me, though, after what we just did?"

I jumped off the couch and helped her up. I put an arm at the back of her knees and the other around her lower back, then lifted her effortlessly.

"I like this," she said, bouncing her feet, rubbing them against each other. I went up the staircase leading to the bedrooms.

"Wrong room," she murmured when I stepped inside my bedroom.

"No, that's the right one. You're staying with me every night from now on."

"Okay."

She sounded vulnerable. I knew exactly how she felt. This thing between us was changing rapidly, and we hadn't even managed to work through all our history, let alone contemplate the future.

"I want to take a shower, actually," she said. "Sorry I didn't tell you earlier."

"No problem. Let's go together."

She bit her lip, looking up at me.

"Don't tell me you want me to shower alone."

"I don't know. This is new. I don't know how to do this."

"Babe, just tell me what you feel comfortable with, and I'll do that. Although, if we do shower together, I can share some more of my skills." I winked.

"You do make a convincing argument. Besides, I could use you to thoroughly wash my back."

I threw my head back, laughing. "I'd be happy to be your shower boy."

"That sounds dirty."

"I didn't mean it like that, but we can make it as dirty as you want."

Giggling, she ran back down the stairs and into the bathroom.

She looked at me over her shoulder as she stepped into the shower and turned on the water.

"I thought the whole point of this was to clean up, not get even dirtier."

"That's debatable," I replied.

As promised, I helped her scrub her back, although I didn't keep my hands only to that area. Not by a long shot. I made sure she was thoroughly clean everywhere.

"Hell yeah. This is the life," Avery muttered.

Once we washed away the soap, I turned off the water.

"I like seeing you like this," I said. "Relaxed in the shower after you've just used my shampoo. You smell like me. I don't want this to stop."

I noticed her swallowing hard. Her eyes were vulnerable.

My whole body seemed to freeze in the time it took her to look from her hands up to me. "I don't want this to stop either, but what if we don't work out again?"

I wrapped my hand in her wet hair, looking her straight in the eyes.

"Avery, we're not the same people we were back then. We're not kids anymore. This is different. We're adults. We're independent. We can make our own choices. We can choose each other."

"Alana will be happy to know that you really do say all the right things all the time."

I laughed, letting go, and we both stepped out. "Alana knows a lot of stuff about us, huh?"

"I need to run what's happening in my life by someone. I've missed having a best friend who knows me inside out."

"As long as Alana is in my corner, I'm all for it."

She wrapped a huge towel around herself. It swallowed her whole. "I can get you a smaller one," I said.

"Oh no, I like this. It's super cozy. It's almost like having on a robe. So, back to Alana," she said as she grabbed another towel and dried her hair with it. "What would you do if she wasn't on your side?"

"Win her over," I said instantly.

"You say that like you'd have no trouble doing it."

I winked at her. "I have good skills when it comes to making people like me."

"Does that mean you would ply her with food as well?"

I leaned into her. "No, Avery. That was just for you. I don't do that for anyone else."

She licked her lips, flashing me a smile. It was unrestrained, innocent, and simply happy, and I'd put it there.

Mission accomplished.

SAM

"Good work, Maxwell," Bobby, one of my colleagues, said as we both entered the doctors' lounge.

"Back at you," I replied.

It had been an exhausting and grueling day, but at least we hadn't lost any patients. That always meant it was a good day. All I wanted to do was grab an energy drink and a vending machine sandwich, shower, and leave.

I stood in front of the vending machine, toying with the card in my pocket. Everything looked like crap.

"Maxwell."

I turned around at Robinson Matthew's voice. He'd just come in. In fact, he was still holding the door open.

"Come to my office," he said. "I've got some news for you."

I instantly felt wide awake, as if I'd already drunk the energy drink. I tried to read from his expression which way this conversation would go, but I was too exhausted to figure it out.

My family always said they were in awe of my people-reading skills. Right now, though, I wouldn't mind some of my legendary skills kicking in. No such luck. I was too tired.

I followed Robinson through the corridors, all the way to his office. The hospital was eerily quiet in the late evening hours. Most patients were asleep, unlike during the day when they were wide awake and being tended to.

I was anticipating Robinson's news. Two weeks ago, we'd spoken about my plans for a clinic, and I hadn't heard anything since.

He guided me inside his office, pointing to the seat opposite him. He sat down behind his desk, and his shoulders sank. That was my first clue. "They don't want it, do they?"

"It's more complicated than that."

"You can just be up front with me. I know how to take a no."

"That's just it, though. It's not exactly a no."

I narrowed my eyes, leaning farther back in the seat, putting the ankle of my right leg on top of my left knee. "What does it mean?"

"It means they are interested in a clinic."

"That's great news." I was certain I could set it up with very little capital. My heart was thumping harder as I contemplated the next steps. "If it's a matter of funds, I can always chip in."

"Maxwell." His voice was hard. "I've told you repeatedly. Never throw your personal money at a state hospital. It's a losing game, trust me. If you're so intent on blowing your trust fund, build your own damn private hospital."

"Setting up a hospital from the ground up is a nightmare," I said. "The paperwork alone would take my entire lifetime. I'm a doctor, not a businessman. What else did the board say?"

"They're opening a satellite hospital in Maine. They would be able to include a clinic there."

I felt as if someone had punched me in the face. "In Maine?"

"Yes. I know this is not ideal."

"What do you mean, not ideal? It's not what I asked for. If they can open one there, then why not here?"

He massaged his temples, like a headache was brewing. "Because that one is being built from the ground up. The layout is flexible. Everything is still flexible. Apparently trying to do something here is too daunting for them to consider."

"I'll talk to them."

"No." He stood up. I'd pissed him off, but I couldn't help it. This was important not only to me, but to the community, and it would help so many people. Besides, I was a Maxwell and used to getting what I wanted. "You listen to me, Maxwell. I like you, but this is my goddamn hospital, and you will not go over my head, got it?"

"I'm sorry. That's not what I meant. I just know that if I pitch it to them, I can convince them. Surely they'd understand how beneficial this would be to the underprivileged in the area."

"You think I haven't pitched this well enough to the board? That's all I've been doing for the past two damn months. They're not budging. There's no profit in a clinic, and the board is leery of building it here. In Maine, they have a larger budget. When starting a hospital from scratch, they can design a section specifically for the clinic and all its needs. Sorry, Sam, but it's Maine or nothing. That's their final say on the matter. Think about it. They don't need an answer right away."

I stood up. Needless to say, I was not happy, though I didn't want to be irrational either. I'd give it time. "When do they need to know?"

"A month, give or take."

"Okay, I'll think about it."

"I know you. You're a hothead, but don't discard it. It's a great opportunity. And with a new hospital being opened, there will be no egos to toss aside, no cliques to fit in. You know how hospitals can get. Everyone on the team will be a fresh hire."

"I know. It definitely has its perks, but it wasn't what I wanted."

"I've emailed you the list of doctors they want to pull in. Big names."

"You think they'll convince them?"

"They stand a good chance." He pointed at me again. "Don't discard this opportunity."

"I won't."

"I can already see you're rolling your eyes into the back of your head."

I held up my hand in defense. "What can I say? I wasn't expecting this. I was looking for a yes or a no. Not a 'Here's our offer in fucking *Maine.*'"

He chuckled at that and said, "You got a yes but with a twist. Flexibility isn't your thing, is it?"

I shrugged. It wasn't something we Maxwells were known for, that was true. "Thank you for everything you've done. See you tomorrow."

"See you, Maxwell."

My mind was spinning while I changed in the locker room. Robinson was right. I couldn't just discard this. An opportunity like it wouldn't come my way again. I was certain there wouldn't be a second chance to build a clinic. Having the option to start one at a brand-new hospital was a once-in-a-lifetime chance these days.

After leaving, I was restless. I did my laps, completing my five miles, but my head was still spinning. I needed more than a run tonight. I didn't want to go home like this. Avery would be there, sensing something wasn't right, and I didn't want to bother her with my confusion. We were just figuring things out; there was no need to put this kind of pressure on her, or on our relationship, for that matter.

I knew just what I needed—the Maxwell gang. My first impulse was to write in the WhatsApp group. I was still new to it. My cousins set me up when we'd had lunch, though I typically had to skip most of the conversations because they happened while I was on shift, and I always put my phone on airplane mode.

I decided to simply call Kimberly.

"Hey, cousin," I said when she answered.

"Hello, Sam."

"Do you have plans tonight?"

"Why? Do you need my help staging a successful date again?"

I laughed. "I wasn't staging it."

"That's what I call it, because... you know what? Never mind. Why do you ask?"

"Got some news at work, and I could use the Maxwell perspective."

"Okay, I'm on it. Just to make it clear, when you say Maxwell perspective, do you mean just me? Me and Reese? Me and everyone else?"

"I'd like as many opinions as possible."

"Wow. I didn't think I'd ever hear someone say that. Tell me you didn't screw things up with Avery already."

"I told you it's about work."

"Hmm. Okay. You can always write in the WhatsApp group."

"Honestly, it moves so fast that it boggles my mind."

She laughed. "Then I'm on it. Want to come to the hotel? Travis and Reese are here already, but I think Travis is going to go home soon. Anyway, we can all go to the bar."

"Sure."

My brothers used to hang out at the bar in the building where they all had their offices, but ever since Travis opened the hotel, it kind of became the family's new headquarters.

On the way to the hotel, I did glance in the WhatsApp group. There were already sixteen new messages, and I scrolled through them. All my brothers were going to be there. Good. I was hoping they would bring their better halves, but that was too much to ask because this was very short notice.

There was a lot going on in the lobby of the Maxwell Hotel

when I arrived. It looked like a new group of tourists was waiting to check in, but the receptionist nodded at me. The staff here already knew the members of the family.

"Everyone's at the bar," he mouthed.

I nodded as a thank-you, then took the staircase, needing the exercise despite the run around the hospital. Upstairs, I scanned the bar for my family. It looked much like the rest of the hotel, a mix of modern tones that had a twenties vibe in smoky gold colors. I usually liked that the space was dark and the lights were dim—it made everything intimate—but tonight, it was so busy that it made it hard to see my family. But that meant business was good for my brother. I was happy for him. He was doing a great thing keeping the family legacy going.

I finally noticed them in the corner to the right of the bar. Declan rose from the group, meeting me halfway through the room.

"Hey, brother," he said.

"Thanks for coming. By the way, did you have a chance to look over Avery's contract?" She'd emailed it to me a while ago, and I immediately forwarded it to Declan.

"Yes. Even I can't find any loopholes, unfortunately. And I also looked into her ex-business partner, Sophia, like you asked me to."

"And?"

"At first glance, nothing seems shady. Although she is about to open a store in New York. I think we know where she got the money from."

"Fuck that. Can't we do something about it?"

"Not yet. We need more info about her new business."

"Right. Keep me posted, okay?"

"Sure. Let's join the others."

I nodded.

"No one came with their better half, huh?" I asked as we approached them. They'd put several small tables together.

Travis sighed. "We leave our families at home, and this is how he repays us."

"It's the best we could do with the short notice, brother," Tyler said.

"We were concerned when Kimberly wrote in the group." That came from Declan. He sat opposite me, frowning.

"So tell us. Also, what do you need to drink?" Tate asked.

I shook my head. "Nothing. What are you all drinking?"

Everyone had a glass in front of them.

"Okay, so he didn't ask for tequila," Tyler said. "That means it's not that bad."

"What?" I asked.

"We were just wondering how bad things are and started taking guesses by what you were going to order. Declan went with Jack and Coke, and I with tequila."

"Interesting choices," I replied.

"Come on. I can't take the suspense anymore," Reese said. "I can't believe you didn't give us a heads-up. You've never asked for a family council, so this has to be big."

"Okay. So I told you I spoke to the hospital's CEO about doing a pro bono clinic," I started.

"Yes," Reese said. "Don't tell me they said no."

"Not exactly. They're opening a new hospital in Maine and say they could build the clinic there."

Tate looked at me with a stern expression. Declan cocked an eyebrow.

"You're not moving to fucking Maine." Surprisingly, that came from Kimberly.

I looked at her. "Yeah, I don't particularly like that option either. I told the CEO I could talk to the board and convince them to do things my way. He didn't appreciate it."

Reese laughed, running a hand through her hair. "Oh, cousin. Every man in this family seems to feel the need to show everyone how big their balls are."

I almost choked at my cousin's description of me and my brothers.

"You know you have a problem respecting authority," Kimberly added.

"No, I don't," I said. Oh yes, I fucking did. She had a point.

"I swear to God, if you leave again, I'm going to..." Reese pressed her lips together. "Okay, I don't know yet what I'm going to do, but I'll definitely do something to stop it. What does Avery have to say about this?"

"Yeah, what does she say?" Kimberly asked.

"I haven't talked to her yet. I had literally just spoken to the CEO before calling you, Kim."

"Why the hell don't you build your own hospital?" Tate asked. "You certainly have the money, and if you need more, we all have untouched trust funds."

I cleared my throat. "I've never used the trust fund."

"This seems like a worthy cause," Declan said.

I looked at Tyler, who was staring intently at me, but he didn't say anything. He was the one who understood me most because we both chose professions where the Maxwell legacy didn't help. Quite the contrary. Most people in med school thought I only got there because of my last name. He'd had similar issues when he was drafted to his NHL team.

"I've always liked keeping my work separate from the Maxwell legacy," I finally replied.

"It's almost like he's ashamed of us," Travis said. "I hope that's not the case or I'm going to take a page out of Reese's book, only not to keep you here, but to get back at you. You know I'm good at that."

I smiled lazily. "You used to be better. You didn't need time to think about it before."

"Dude, I have a newborn. I don't sleep. I'm slower these days."

"There's also another problem," I said. "I'm a doctor, not a businessman, and I don't want to deal with everything that opening a clinic involves."

Travis looked around the table. "If only you had a gazillion Maxwells who were businesspeople to help you out, you know? We have *a lot* of connections."

Reese and Kimberly both straightened in their seats. Tate nodded.

Declan spoke first. "I can help with anything regarding legal stuff. There will be a lot of it when you start, but I'm definitely up for it."

"We each have different skills," Tate said. "We all started our businesses from the ground up."

I shook my head. "True, but you don't have time for this."

"We can make time," Tate replied instantly.

"You're going to have a baby, Tate," I reminded him. "This is not the time to take more things on."

I looked at Travis. "I really appreciate the offer, but it's not the way to go."

"I have time," Luke said.

"You have an architecture company," I pointed out.

"It's called interchangeable skills."

Tate cleared his throat, and everyone at the table was silent. I had a flashback to our childhood when he would do the same when he wanted our attention. I was happy that some things never changed.

"Listen, obviously we all have lives and businesses, but that doesn't mean we can't come together for a project like this. Just know that you can count on us. At the very least, we can help you put a team in place so you don't have to do any managerial tasks."

"I hadn't thought about that," I said. I didn't envy the CEO's job. He spent a lot of time dealing with paperwork.

"Yeah, we'd do anything to keep you here," Reese said, batting her eyelashes. "I would even leave Travis for you in case you wanted full-time employees who don't need to be paid."

"Yeah, me too," Kimberly said.

"What the hell is this?" Travis asked. "Are you two striking or something?"

"No, we're just saying we can migrate to Sam if he needs us more than you do."

"I worked for like half a year to convince you both to join me," Travis exclaimed.

Reese smiled sheepishly. "Awwww. You'd miss us."

I laughed. "Girls, you don't have to leave Travis for me, but I appreciate that you would."

"When are you going to tell Avery?" Reese asked. She sounded serious.

"After I think this through. I don't want to just throw it out there. I don't want her to worry about anything."

"Just don't wait too long, okay?" Kimberly said.

"I think it's best to discuss things as they happen," Tate chipped in unexpectedly. He usually didn't give any sort of relationship advice. Then again, I hadn't been in a relationship when I was in Chicago. I could imagine that, over the years, he'd had to hone that skill what with everyone getting hitched.

"You decide when you tell her," Reese said. "In the meantime, I'd appreciate it if you would also call me for help when you need ideas or, you know, minions to arrange your dates."

Kimberly balked. "I'm not a minion."

"I'd like to be one. I can't believe you didn't call me."

"Deal." I'd forgotten how to navigate family relationships. It was true that Kimberly and I spoke the most when we were away from Chicago. We bonded over the fact that we were separated from the family. "Reese, I swear."

She raised an eyebrow. "On your heart?"

"I promise I'll call you too."

"Okay, now I'm happy," Reese said, and then her face broke into a smile. "You know, I've always loved cozy blankets. I imagine that's where Kimberly got the idea."

Kimberly and I both started laughing, realizing what Reese needed. She wanted credit too.

It just so happened that I planned to woo Avery with a lot more dates, so Reese would have plenty of time to help me out too.

AVERY

On a Thursday morning, I got the surprise of my life when I opened my Etsy inbox. I had a message from Sophia. Why had she even tracked me down? I was using my legal name as a seller, so I guess it wasn't rocket science to find me. Just shocking that she'd *want* to.

Avery, hey, what a quaint shop you've got here. I'm glad I found you. I'm throwing an opening party for my new store in New York. I've decided to put myself out there. You're welcome to come.

She listed her website in the signature.

For a few seconds, I couldn't breathe. I blinked rapidly.

Am I seeing wrong? Is this for real? She stole all the money from the company to fund her own business?

With a shaky hand, I opened the website. I couldn't believe she'd done it. She was selling designer shoes—and *jewelry*. I bit my lip, clicking on the Event page. The official opening party was in two weeks.

I was too stunned to think. Here I was trying to rebuild my life from scratch, and there she was, financing everything with the money she took from *my* business.

My God, is life ever fair?

No, no, no. I can't go down that route. It won't help anything.

I took a deep breath, but I was shaking. When stuff like this happened, I liked to remind myself of everything I had and all the good things that had happened to me. Mom was healthy. I'd reconnected with Sam. I'd found my passion for handmade jewelry. I had plenty of things to be happy about and grateful for.

But I couldn't let this go. Sophia was literally rubbing this in my face, so I made a split-second decision. I was going to attend her stupid party. She obviously wanted to pour salt in the wound, but I bet she didn't expect me to actually go. Not in a million years. I wasn't the one in the wrong here, and I had no reason to hide. I had all the reason to call her out, and I sure as shit was going to do that. I'd made a stupid mistake, and I owned up to it, but that didn't mean I would let her simply get away with everything.

Besides, I had another reason for wanting to attend. I needed to warn her potential business partners about her. I couldn't live with myself if I simply sat back and let her scam someone else.

I stood up, shaking out my legs and my hands. I was jittery, and I had too much adrenaline to sit down and continue working.

Fuck this.

Fuck Sophia.

This isn't fair. It isn't right.

I couldn't calm down, but I still had to finish this jewelry set and get it to the post office.

Taking a few deep breaths, I pulled myself together. I could make a voodoo doll or imagine all the ways I could make her pay *after* I finished and shipped the order. I wanted my new clients to feel like they were special and could count on me to deliver on time.

Grudgingly, I sat down and then plugged in my earbuds, playing relaxing nature sounds. I chose one with a waterfall.

Thirty seconds later, I realized Zen music wasn't going to help me, so I opened Spotify to the newest hits.

Yep, that's it. Blasting Taylor Swift and Adele in my eardrums was doing the trick.

I finished the jewelry an hour later. It was gorgeous—a mix of gold and silver with pearls as the centerpiece. It was the most beautiful wedding jewelry I'd seen. I packed the pieces in a beautiful pink box that I'd also ordered off Etsy—I liked supporting other small businesses. Once the box was ready, I practically ran to the post office, which was only open for another half hour.

Knowing I was doing everything by myself gave me a sense of accomplishment. I didn't have to rely on anyone again. But could I scale this up? Was it financially viable? I didn't really need much to live on, but I wanted to have a healthy nest egg just in case Mom got sick again.

I was out of breath by the time I stepped inside the post office. The clerk was mildly annoyed that I came in ten minutes before closing time, but he processed my order, and I was on my way a couple minutes later.

I walked back home at a slow pace, still out of breath from my sprint. My thoughts circled back to Sophia. I truly couldn't believe her audacity.

To my astonishment, when I arrived at the loft, Sam was already there, leaning on the kitchen counter and drinking a glass of water.

"Hi, beautiful. Where were you?"

"I went to the post office to ship my order."

"What's wrong? You look tense."

I rolled my shoulders, attempting to smile. "Picked up on that, huh?"

"Yeah." He narrowed his eyes.

"What?"

"I was going to take you out today."

"Where?"

"That's the thing. I haven't decided. Reese was determined to give me some input."

He came to me, taking off my beanie and my jacket. I always liked that he did that. His real intent was just to touch me, but I didn't mind. Not one bit. I loved the possessiveness of his actions.

"She suggested a ride on the Centennial Wheel," he continued. "Apparently it's got some glass-bottomed gondolas. Or we could do a tour of Michigan Avenue by horse."

I wrinkled my nose.

He chuckled. "But none of those things felt like you."

"They're not," I replied, giddy that he knew me so well.

"Besides, I didn't want this gorgeous ass to freeze in a carriage." He paused before adding, "Come on, tell me what happened. Then I'll make new plans based on that."

"Sophia messaged me on Etsy today. She's opening a new store in New York with my money."

"Fuck!" Sam exclaimed.

"My thoughts exactly."

"Declan told me something about it."

I quirked a brow. "He did?"

"Yeah. I asked if he looked over your contract with her, and he said there's nothing he can do about it. He also said to keep an eye on her business once she opens it. Maybe there will be something there he can use to get your money back."

"She just wants to rub it in my face, thinks she can walk all over me, but she can't. So I want to go to the opening party. It's in two weeks."

Sam looked at me intently. "Are you sure?"

"Yes."

"You're bold. I like that."

I smiled sheepishly. "I like it too. I didn't know I had it in me."

"Can you take a plus-one?"

My eyes widened. "You want to come with me?"

"Hell yes. I want to be right beside you, babe."

"Hey, having you as my arm candy will be a plus for me too. You're definitely coming," I said with a grin.

"And now I know what we'll do. I'll take you out on a date while we're in New York."

"That sounds fabulous. I've never been. Ah, there are so many places in the world I'd like to see."

"Like where?" He touched the side of my face and put a hand at the small of my back, pressing me into him.

"I'd really like to see Paris one day. I wasn't just saying that to Kimberly to make conversation."

"I'll take you anywhere you want, babe."

I sighed. "You mean that, don't you?"

"Hell yes. Now that you're mine again, I plan to spoil you all the time. Now, tell me about your day."

"I finished a beautiful set of jewelry, and I can't wait for my customer to get it. I hope they're happy. I'm really digging this, but I'm not used to the pace. It's very different."

"I've always liked that about you, even in high school."

"What exactly?"

"Your mom couldn't buy you the prom dress you wanted. You definitely didn't want *me* to buy the prom dress you wanted. So you waitressed, despite all the pressure from preparing for exams."

I shrugged. "I wanted the dress, and I needed to make it happen without imposing on anyone else. In some ways, we're very much alike. We both go for what we want. I think you're very brave for traveling to countries that are so different from ours. Do you think it influenced your goals of opening a pro bono clinic?"

"Definitely. I never thought about it before joining Doctors Without Borders. It shaped many of my thoughts and beliefs."

His eyes were unfocused for a few seconds, as if he were lost in a memory.

I was immensely happy that he'd spoken about it openly with me, that he wanted me to know. He trusted me.

"I'd like to ask you something… and for you to answer. Why did you leave all those years ago? Why didn't you want me by your side?"

I blinked, suddenly feeling as if my eyes were starting to burn. "It's not that I didn't want you there… but I thought it wasn't fair to you, you know? To ask you to go through all that with me. I think I was afraid you'd fall out of love with me if you had to witness all the hardships that come with the disease. I didn't want to keep you from reaching for your dreams. I wanted you by my side, Sam. Don't ever think I didn't. Does that make sense?"

He nodded. "Yes. Thank you."

"What else do you want to know?"

"Nothing. That's the closure I needed."

My chest felt lighter. I smiled at him, biting my lower lip. "And about tonight," I said, "I have an idea."

"I'm all ears."

"We'll stay home, and I'll take care of you for a change and spoil you and cover you in kisses."

His blue eyes seemed brighter. "I like where this is going. Where are you starting?"

Taking his hand, I led him to the couch, then pushed him down on it. He looked at me hungrily. I climbed into his lap, putting my legs on either side of his thighs and kneeling.

"Where *should* I start?" I purred.

"Wherever you want, babe."

"No, tonight you get to pick your favorites."

His eyes flashed, and he wiggled his eyebrows.

I pinched his shoulder. "You are *such* a guy."

"What? You asked me to pick my favorite."

"That's right. My fault entirely," I said, moving a bit farther away and opening the button of his jeans.

With a flash, I realized I wanted to do this my whole life. Love him and take care of him and… well, let myself be loved. If I was being honest, that wasn't something I did easily, and I really didn't know why, or if there even was a reason. But I'd fallen hard for Sam all those years ago and again now, and I wasn't afraid.

Life was simply too good, and we were fighting our demons together. I could finally let myself hope that this could last forever. That we'd come home to each other like this and talk, kiss, hug, spoil each other with delicious food, and, of course, sexy times.

SAM

"*P*ity we couldn't fly in Travis's helicopter," I told Avery as we entered our suite at the Plaza Hotel in New York two weeks later.

My brother bought a helicopter a while ago after he sold his first business. He even had a pilot's license, but he didn't have time to fly himself anymore. He couldn't find a pilot for today, so we'd come with the commercial airline.

"That's fine. I enjoyed the plane flight, and it was fun to see LaGuardia." Avery looked around with a huge smile. "This place is so fancy."

I liked making her happy. New York looked festive at this time of the year. Chicago, too, but not like New York. The whole city was lit up. We'd spotted a few Christmas trees during the Uber ride over, though it wasn't even Thanksgiving yet. Retailers were always rushing the holidays.

Avery looked around, biting her lip. "I'll change real quick, and then we can go." The party was in two hours on Amsterdam Avenue.

"We can stroll a bit in the city before the party too," I suggested.

"Only if you agree to be my tour guide."

"Yes, ma'am. At your service."

"I mean, I guess we could also stay inside. It's a pity to have this huge suite and not make use of it. Especially the bed. But I've never seen the city." She tapped a fingertip against her lips. "Decisions, decisions."

She was adorable, fighting with herself.

"Nah, a tour it is," she finally exclaimed.

I changed much faster than Avery—I kept my jeans on but switched from my sweater to a shirt with cuff links. I wore them so rarely that it felt strange buttoning them up.

I was happy that I was going with her tonight. Avery was strong, and I had no doubt she could kick ass on her own, but I wanted her to know she could count on me.

I had yet to talk to her about the clinic. I'd spoken to the CEO again, and he'd finally agreed to let me talk to the board. But when I spoke with them, it didn't go well at all. They said that since they'd already approved the opening of a pro bono clinic in Maine, there was no point doing one in Chicago too. Bottom line, it just wasn't feasible for them.

No matter what my brothers said, I'd prefer a pro bono clinic attached to a big hospital. But I didn't want to go to fucking Maine.

"I'm ready," Avery exclaimed, coming out of the bathroom. She twirled once, smiling from ear to ear. "What do you think?"

She looked stunning in her black dress. It was short and showcased her perfect ass. The caveman inside me was satisfied that her cleavage was well covered by what seemed to be a scarf attached to the dress—I was clueless about stuff like that.

"Babe, you look gorgeous. But you're going to freeze, especially in those shoes."

They were silver heels that looked damn sexy, but they'd be no use outside.

"No, I've got my puffy coat. I'll be fine."

The second we stepped outside the hotel, her teeth started chattering.

"Babe, you're cold. I'm not allowing this."

She cocked a brow. "Allow? Is that the doctor tone coming out?"

I cleared my throat, adjusting my voice. "I don't want you to get sick. Let's do a cab tour."

She laughed but nodded. "You're a genius."

I nodded at the doorman, who flagged a cab for us. Once inside, I instructed the driver to go around all the major attractions in the area. We drove by Central Park first.

"Oh my God, the Christmas tree is already up," Avery exclaimed when we passed Rockefeller Center, pressing her nose against the window. "But it's not lit."

"Nah, I think the tree lighting ceremony is sometime after Thanksgiving."

We then passed the Empire State Building. The driver kept pointing out landmarks, but I could tell Avery wasn't truly here with us.

"You're thinking about the party, aren't you?" I asked her.

"Yes. I'm sorry."

"Don't worry. The tour is about to be over anyway. We have to be at the party in twenty minutes."

Obviously, we ran into traffic, so we arrived thirty minutes late. Avery was fidgeting, but she held her chin high as I helped her step out of the cab.

"You know what?" she said with a glint in her eye. "It's actually better that we're a bit late. We get to make a grand entrance this way. Hopefully everyone is already here. I can't wait to see the look on Sophia's face."

I liked her when she was feisty.

We walked arm in arm and entered through the main door.

The shop was small and, in my opinion, not impressive. It looked like any other shoe shop. There were small tables everywhere with champagne flutes. The shop also had jewelry on display, and I had to admit, it looked damn good.

Avery stiffened.

"Babe?" I asked.

Her eyes were glued to where the jewelry was merchandised.

"Those are my designs. She stole my designs," she murmured, clearly in shock.

Fucking hell.

There were probably a dozen people milling around. I spotted Sophia immediately, recognizing her from a picture Avery showed me. Her hair was ridiculous, red, and piled up in what was supposed to be some sort of updo, but she just looked like she had a snake on her head. Her dress was gold. It looked cheap.

She immediately came up to us. "Avery, what are you doing here?"

"You invited me to the opening. I wanted to come check it out," Avery said. Her voice was serene, as if she couldn't possibly understand why Sophia was out of sorts.

"I didn't think you'd actually come!"

Avery smirked. "Why? Are you afraid I might say something inappropriate? What are you going to do, call security? Oh, that's right, you don't have any."

"You can't come into my store—" she started in an aggressive tone.

Time for me to cut in.

"Be civil," I said. "Sam Maxwell. We haven't been introduced."

She stopped midsentence, folding her arms over her chest. "I've heard plenty about you from Avery. I see your taste in women still sucks."

Interesting. Avery mentioned me throughout the years? I made a mental note of that. *Now, Sophia had better prepare herself for my displeasure.*

"Really, you're resorting to that?" I asked, cocking a brow. There was another reason I wanted to come with Avery. No one would mess with her if she had the Maxwell name behind her.

I was a hypocrite where the family name was concerned. I always claimed I didn't want to use it, but I didn't mind if it benefited someone else's situation, especially for Avery's sake. For the first time, I understood why my brothers were so over-protective of their women. It was an instinct. I couldn't help it. I wanted to flat-out protect her from any problems and keep her from harm.

"I see you have investors here," I said. It was an educated guess, considering two of the guys in expensive suits looked like they'd just come from Wall Street.

"Investors, huh?" Avery asked in a high-pitched voice that got the attention of everyone in the room. "Sophia and I used to work together, you know. She swindled me. Can you believe it? I didn't get another lawyer to double-check the contract, so basically each of us was allowed to take as much money out of the business as we wanted for reinvestment or personal use. I never took one cent except the salary we agreed on. She stole close to a quarter-million dollars from the business. And the jewelry you see on display? That's my work. My designs."

Sophia gasped. "Take that back. It's not true. I didn't steal anything." But the look on her face said otherwise.

"I have the bank statements to prove that you transferred money to yourself." Avery looked around the room, gauging the attention of the attendees, then said, "I'm staying at the Plaza for tonight. If anyone needs more information, you can always look for me there. Make sure you have good contracts, legally sound-proof and then some. Though even if you do, don't think that she'll respect them. She's got a talent for slipping out of any binding situations."

"I can sue you for this, you know," Sophia said.

Avery rolled her shoulders back. "Please. Be my guest."

"Get out of here." I could've laughed at the look on Sophia's face.

"My pleasure. I did what I came here to do. I sure as hell won't allow you to steal from anyone else." Avery kept her professional poise, which pissed Sophia off even more. It was amazing.

"Get out," Sophia said through gritted teeth.

"Don't come any closer," I warned.

"I will call the police," she threatened.

"Yes, please do. We're going to have a lovely chat with them," Avery said, shaking slightly. I could tell that, despite her calm appearance, she was seething inside, and I couldn't blame her. She glanced at me when I squeezed her arm.

"Come on, Sam. Let's go. We have a wonderful suite waiting for us."

She held her head high as we walked to the front door. Chatter broke out in the room, obvious panic setting in. Sophia was trying unsuccessfully to quiet it down.

When we stepped out, a few of her guests came with us, saying things like "Thanks for the warning" and "Glad you two arrived before we made a dumb investment."

Avery released a huge sigh once we were alone.

"I'm so proud of you, babe," I said. "Did you plan this?"

"No. I wish I had a diabolical mind, but I don't. When I saw she copied my designs, I think something just snapped inside me. To be honest, I'd simply hoped I could talk to her partners and warn them individually, but it was easier this way. I realized she was going to kick me out one way or another, so I wanted to be quick." She looked at me intently. "Do you think the others will take my warning seriously or just discard me as some crazy person?"

I couldn't believe this woman. She'd come here to warn others just so they wouldn't fall into the same trap she did. I loved every damn inch of her.

"Based on the few who left along with us, I'd say Sophia's

going to have trouble finding investors. But if the others don't believe you, it's their fault. If nothing else, I'm sure they'll do some more research before they invest in her. Do you have the bank statements you mentioned?"

"You bet I do. Just in case, you know."

Good to know. When we got back, I'd give those to Declan. Man, she amazed me, and I had such respect for her and what she'd done.

"Want us to do another cab tour of New York?"

"Honestly, I'd rather we go back to the hotel. I'm super jittery. I think I need a workout."

I kissed her forehead. "Is that code for something?"

She laughed, and I felt her whole body relax. "No, I mean a real workout, but I'm not excluding a sexy one after that. Let's go."

"You don't have to tell me twice, babe."

I'd only been in New York a few times before, and I'd never realized what a shit show the traffic was. Even though we were only a few blocks away, it took us forty minutes to get to the Plaza. Walking would've probably been faster, but Avery would've frozen despite her long coat.

Once inside, she quickly changed and went directly to the fitness area. I stayed in the suite, mindlessly checking the menu of the restaurant where we had dinner reservations. I was of two minds about going after Avery, but then I would distract her from her workout, and she really seemed to need it. I understood that. It was one of the reasons I ran after shifts. I needed to get rid of excess adrenaline. I also sensed that she wanted some alone time to digest all that happened, and I respected that too.

The room phone rang. *Does reception need something from us?* I couldn't imagine who else would call here.

"Hello?" I said.

"Mr. Maxwell, we have someone at the front desk looking for Ms. Avery."

"Who?"

"Sophia Pitt."

I saw red. That viper actually showed up here after what she'd done? She didn't know who she was messing with.

"Send her up to the room, please," I bit out.

"Of course, sir."

I couldn't believe it. I'd stayed out of it at her shop because I wanted Avery to say her piece, but I couldn't believe Sophia had the audacity to show up here.

She knocked a few minutes later, and I immediately opened the door.

"Where's Avery?" she demanded.

"She's not here right now."

"That bitch. I lost investors tonight. I'm going to sue the crap out of her," she seethed, stalking inside the suite. "Where is she? I need to talk to her. She needs to fix this."

"Listen, Sophia. There are two things you need to know about me. One, I would do anything for Avery. And two, I have the whole Maxwell family backing me up. Good contract or not, we'll find ways to crush you."

"Flaunting your family name, huh? Avery always told me you didn't like to brag about your resources."

"I've changed my mind. When it comes to Avery, I will use everything in my power to protect her from people like you."

"People like me? I'm a businesswoman. She just made a bad deal. She doesn't get to bad-mouth me."

"Fuck yes, she does. My brother Declan is a lawyer. You don't want him on your case. Be thankful that bad-mouthing you is all Avery did." Once I gave Declan proof that she'd stolen designs—intellectual property—he should be able to hand Sophia her ass in a lawsuit. I personally couldn't wait.

"All she did? Did you hear what I said? I lost investors."

"And you'll lose more than that if you don't fuck off and pay back every single cent you stole." I was pissed. How dare she?

She burst out laughing, but her eyes were attentive as she looked me up and down.

"You deserve someone smarter than Avery, and much better-looking." She opened her coat and then dropped it on the bed, pulling down the zipper of her dress. "Someone like me."

"What the fuck are you doing?"

23

AVERY

I dried my face with a towel as I slowly walked down the corridor back to the suite. Now I understood why people went running when they were stressed out. I was prepared to order a treadmill-desk combo from Amazon as soon as we got home.

I still had a ton of adrenaline in my body. I couldn't believe I ran my mouth like that at the shop. As a general rule, I didn't like to make a spectacle of myself or throw others under the bus, but the thought that Sophia could rob someone else made my blood boil.

I swiped my card, pushing the door of the suite open, and then I froze.

What the hell? Why is Sophia here?

My heart dropped. The zipper of her dress was undone. I could see the side of her boob from the doorway.

Sam was red in the face and clearly angry.

"You get the hell out of here," he bellowed.

"Why should I?"

"What the hell?" I said, walking up to them.

Both looked at me in surprise.

Sam shook his head. "Babe, I've got this. I'm calling security to escort her out."

"You fucking bitch," I exclaimed. "You think you can just throw yourself at my man?"

"Oh please. If he knows what's good for him, he'll drop your sorry ass anyway. You're a killjoy. And you need to get your shit together. My investors dropped me."

"Means they know what's good for them." I was so angry, I could barely breathe. I balled my hands into fists.

She scoffed. "It's not my fault you blindly trusted my lawyer."

"I thought you were my friend, not some two-bit scammer."

"Sophia, I told you, we have a very good lawyer in the family," Sam said in a calm voice.

"I see. You're going to let him fight your battles, huh?" Sophia said, crossing her arms over her chest.

"No, I will publicly declare everything. I will lay it out for any of your investors to read."

"You bitch."

I smiled sardonically. I really didn't know I had this in me.

"You don't get to call me names or make my life any harder than you already have." I felt some of my anger seep out as well as the resentment I'd been holding on to ever since the business collapsed. "Do you have any idea how hard it was for me to start over from scratch, to keep my mother from worrying?" It was my deepest fear that if Mom worried too much about me, she might get sick again. I read online that when you're stressed out, the body produces cortisol, which blocks the immune system.

"I don't give a crap." Her snotty reply infuriated me.

I was shaking. She'd thrown herself at Sam. This had to be rock bottom, even for her.

I walked to the door and opened it. "Leave, Sophia, or I swear to God, I'll lose my shit, and you won't even have a dress to walk out in."

She huffed, taking her coat from the bed. She'd put it on our *bed*! I had to dig my nails into my palms to keep from slapping her. I held my breath when she walked past me; I'd had enough of her sickly sweet perfume back at the store.

Once she left, I turned to Sam.

"You were magnificent," he said.

"Why was her zipper undone?"

He put his hand on his hips, his feet wide apart. "She threw herself at me. Obviously failed."

"Did she kiss you... or did anything else happen?"

My heart was in my throat, and I could barely breathe.

In an instant, Sam was next to me. "No, babe. Why would you even think that?"

"I don't know. I came in, she was half naked, and you were red in the face." My voice shook.

"Because I was pissed off, and I told her to fucking get dressed. I'd never touch another woman. You're everything I want, okay? I'm here *for* you and *with* you, and that's never going to change."

He put a hand at the back of my neck, resting his thumb at the base of my hairline. Tilting his head forward, he touched his forehead to mine. "Don't doubt me, Avery."

"I don't," I whispered. "I just... I don't know. She's hurt me so much, and then seeing her here with her boob hanging out. It messed with my brain."

"You mean the world to me, Avery. Let me show that to you." He brought his other hand just under my shirt, skimming his thumb on the waistline of my pants.

"You can't do that," I whispered, taking a step back.

"What?"

"I'm super sweaty. I need to shower first."

With a wicked grin, he put his hands on my shoulders, flipping me around and leading me to the bathroom. "Let's take that shower together."

"That's right. We can start on that post-workout workout."

He came closer until I felt his hot breath in my ear. "Avery, I want to wipe everything from your mind except how much I want you and how much you mean to me."

I shivered. "It's already working," I assured him.

I loved the shower. It was huge, and a walk-in.

Sam made quick work of discarding my workout clothes. I, on the other hand, needed a while to get all the buttons on his shirt open. I managed to finally undo all of them, including the cuff links, and then pushed it down his gorgeous biceps, drinking him in. He was sexy even just wearing an undershirt, but I preferred him buck naked, so I quickly took that off as well.

"Sometimes I still can't believe these muscles," I murmured, slowly drawing my fingers over his abs, playing on all the ridges before tackling his belt. Somehow, I managed to muck it up, and he took over, immediately unbuckling it. His pants and boxers landed on the floor almost instantly afterward.

I turned on the water, loving the hot spray, grateful it was washing the sweat off my skin. He covered my mouth with his, pushing us both deeper into the shower. The water was hot enough that steam was rising up. Even the tiles were warm as he flattened my back against them. He moved his mouth all over my neck, then went down to my breasts, looking up at me while he teased wide circles around my nipples, first the right one and then the left. Then he skimmed his thumbs over both of them as he trailed a path downward with his mouth.

He'd barely gotten me naked, and I was already starving for him.

Today had taken a toll on me, there were no two ways about it, but being here with him was everything I needed.

He looked me straight in the eyes, coming back up my body again, raining kisses everywhere. He paid even more attention to my nipples, pressing the flat of his tongue against them. I rolled my hips forward.

"This is so good," I murmured.

He kissed farther up my body before straightening up and looking me in the eyes. "I'm yours, Avery."

I shivered despite the hot water. He dropped both hands onto the sides of my body, drawing his fingers from my waist down to my hips and then back up. The light touch brought me to tremors. He looked at me through hooded eyelids before kissing me long and deep and wet. I gripped the railing of the shower, needing to ground myself a bit.

This was the effect Sam Maxwell had on me. Every time he kissed me, my world spun almost literally.

He explored me with patience and precision, and I was already dripping wet for him. My thighs were weak, and so were my knees. I rolled my hips and cried out when my clit collided with his cock. His erection was trapped between us. Feeling the length of him against my entrance sent shock waves of pleasure through me.

He groaned against my mouth, moving his hips back and forth, rubbing against me and driving me crazy. It was satisfying, and yet at the same time, it spurred my hunger. God, how I needed him. I thought I was wet and ready before, but now I was positively dripping.

Sam groaned against my mouth again and then brought his lips to my ear. "Damn, Avery, I can do this all night long, all my life, baby."

My skin broke out in goose bumps.

"Sam," I muttered.

He rubbed the tip of his cock right against my clit, and I couldn't think anymore. I was one huge ball of fire and hunger. I squeezed my eyes shut, trying to ground myself, but then he pushed inside me. I let go of the shower railing and gripped his shoulders instead.

"Sam!"

"I'm going to lift you in my arms, babe. I need a better angle."

I just nodded; I couldn't even speak past the intense sensations rippling through me. I felt him lift me by my ass, and then he started pounding for real. He was right—the angle was so much better this way. My legs were wider because I was holding them at his sides. His expression changed from turned on to consumed by pleasure as he thrust inside me.

He moved one hand away from my waist, touching my left breast before lowering his fingers to my clit, brushing it between thrusts. I nearly passed out from the intense sensations. Between the hot water, his fingers, and his cock, I was completely lost to him. He increased the pressure on my clit while I tried to kiss his shoulder and his arm. But I couldn't even do that. With every wave of heat and need coiling through me, I was less in control of my body. My muscles contracted and loosened repeatedly. My skin was on fire. My pussy was on edge.

I badly needed to come.

I exploded the next second and held on tight to him, riding the wave until I was completely spent. Only then did he slow his thrusts, murmuring in my ear, "You're amazing and beautiful, babe. And I'm not done making you come tonight."

My brain barely registered what he said, but my body reacted instantly, my inner muscles pulsing.

He groaned and abruptly turned off the water.

"What are you doing?" I murmured.

"I need you someplace else," he said, lowering me to the floor. We toweled off quickly.

As we reached the bed, he kissed my right shoulder. He brought a hand to my pussy, strumming his fingers over my sensitive flesh. I nearly lost my balance.

"I'm right here, babe," he whispered in my ear, pressing three fingers against my clit.

I dropped my head back, resting it on his shoulder, feeling his cock between my thighs. I reached down, cupping him and pressing the length of his erection against my entrance. My entire body pulsed.

"Fuuck! Avery!"

Flipping me around, he laid me down at the edge of the bed, pushing me onto my back. My knees and feet were up in the air. He leaned over me, drawing the tip of his nose up my neck at the same time that he rubbed his cock against my entrance. It instantly spurred me to tremors.

How can he bring me to the edge so fast?

Raising his head, he looked around. I realized he needed a pillow, so I handed him one. He shoved it under my ass the next second, lifting me to a higher angle. When he entered me, I squeezed my eyes shut. He let out a long, primal groan.

"Avery... fuck, you feel so good, babe."

My inner muscles clamped around him even more intensely than before. I knew he was close. I felt his cock pulse inside me. He was moving too slowly, so I planted my heels on the bed and tried to roll my hips faster. Then I felt both of his hands at my sides, slowing me.

"No, babe. I want you to come again. I want to feel you around my cock before I climax."

His words turned me on almost as much as feeling him inside me.

He put one knee on the bed, leaning over me and kissing my nipples. He'd almost stilled all his movements now. When he brought a hand to my clit, I knew I wouldn't last long. The sensation completely undid me, and I came even faster than before. Through my thrashing and crying out, I felt him change the rhythm. He chased his own climax until his whole body shuddered on a long orgasm that seemed to tear through him.

He smiled down at me, even though his face was still slightly contorted and red from his release. The veins in his temples and neck were pulsing. He put both knees on the bed and took the pillow out from under my ass.

I moved to the center of the bed, patting a spot next to me. "I think we should both lie down."

He laughed, collapsing on the bed. "Fuck, that was good."

"I agree."

He was on his back, arms bent at the elbow, hands under his head, drawing in deep breaths. The red in his face was slowly fading. Blinking his eyes open, he glanced at me. In an instant, he turned onto his side and pushed himself up on an elbow. He moved closer, kissing my cheek, then going up to my ear.

"You're amazing. And I'm so lucky to be here with you."

I laughed nervously and pulled back.

"I mean it," he added.

I bit my lower lip. "How can you say that? This afternoon's been a shit show."

"About the afternoon. Why didn't you tell me you were in so much debt?"

"Because it wouldn't have made a difference. Now that you do know, I'm very embarrassed."

"You shouldn't be. Someone took advantage of your goodwill. I can make it go away, babe."

"What? The embarrassment?"

"No. The debt."

I froze. "No. Absolutely not. It's my fuckup. I have to clean it up."

"Life doesn't have to be hard. Just let me do this—"

"No. Really. It's not up for discussion. Why would you even suggest that?"

"Because I love you, Avery. And I want to be right next to you. Even on shit-show days. Especially on those, actually, because I know it's good for you to have me by your side."

I swooned completely, but I was still tripped up by the first part. "You love me?"

He smiled wickedly. "You know I do."

I shrugged, feeling shy all of a sudden. "I'd hoped."

He shifted, grabbing my hips and flipping us over so I was straddling him.

I propped my hands on his shoulders. "In case you didn't know, I love you too," I said. My face was hurting from grinning so widely.

"Really, huh?"

I nodded. "Yes. So damn much."

I slid forward a bit and sat on him, realizing he was semihard again. "How is this even possible?"

He wiggled his eyebrows. "I told you, I want to do this"—he pointed between us—"our whole life. And I'm going to prove it to you."

"We're not going to explore New York at all, are we?"

He grinned. "Not tonight."

SAM

"You're sure your parents won't mind that I'm only bringing pumpkin pie?" Avery asked, shifting her weight from one foot to the other.

"No one's expecting you to bring anything. Mom cooked enough food to feed everyone."

"That's not the point. It's Thanksgiving. I don't like showing up empty-handed."

"You're not."

I came home from the hospital ten minutes ago and was shell-shocked that the whole house smelled like pumpkin pie.

"I didn't know you could bake."

Avery blushed. "I can't. I spent half the day with Mom on the phone, following her instructions. I did a test batch before this one, and it was complete shit. I threw it away. But this one actually looks good."

"Fuck, I love you so damn much."

She grinned, coming closer. She was already dressed to go, wearing a red sweater dress and black tights. Rising on her toes, she put her arms around my neck. "Sam Maxwell, if it gets this reaction out of you, I'll bake more often."

I kissed the right corner of her mouth. She tasted faintly like sugar. I wanted to eat her up.

Taking a step back, I grabbed the pie she'd carefully packed for transport on the kitchen island, then pointed to the door. "Let's go. We don't want to be late. Mom insists on waiting for everyone to be present before she cuts the turkey."

"Okay."

She grabbed a bag she'd placed by the door before we headed out.

"What's that?" I asked, pointing to it.

"Oh, I spoke with Kimberly about my jewelry. A few of the girls want some."

I'm going to owe Kimberly for life! She was a genius. Avery's business was moving slowly, and she was vehemently against any financial help from me. However, when we returned from New York, I spoke to Declan, and Avery sent him the bank statements and the documents proving she'd designed the products Sophia was selling in her store. I was determined to do anything in my power to help her go after that woman.

* * *

WE ARRIVED AT MY PARENTS' house in time for dinner. By the looks of it, we were the first ones; there were no cars in the driveway. My parents waited for us at the entrance.

"Oh, honey, it's so good to see you," Mom said, hugging Avery, who instantly wrapped her arms around my mom's back in a hug and leaned into her touch. The two of them had always been close, or at least that was how it had seemed to me.

"It's great to see you again," Dad added.

"Lena, Emmett, you both look great. I brought a pumpkin pie."

Mom smiled. "Darling, you shouldn't have, but I'm glad you did. I love pumpkin pie. I'll take it to the kitchen."

"I'm coming with you. I want to help," Avery said.

"Oh, there's nothing for you to do. The table in the dining room is already set. I've brought out all the food except the turkey. I'm waiting for everyone to sit down first. What's in that bag?"

"Some samples for jewelry."

Mom winked. "Kimberly told me all about it. I looked at your Etsy store. It's fabulous. Sign me up for at least a pair of earrings."

Avery grinned. "Will do."

"Now, you two go relax. I'll join you in a minute."

I chuckled as Mom headed to the kitchen.

"Lena is usually easygoing about our gatherings. She makes us take turns working at the kitchen island, or if we go into the yard, everyone just grabs a plate and cutlery for themselves," Dad said.

"That's smart."

"You've got to get creative with so many people," he continued. "But she wants to do it all by herself on Thanksgiving."

"I know your family gatherings were always overwhelming."

"Now more than ever, since all my boys have a better half."

"Do you think the others will be late?" I asked.

"No. Look, there are three cars pulling into the driveway," Dad remarked, glancing out the window.

Kimberly and Reese got out of one, along with Declan and Liz. Travis and Bonnie emerged from another, carrying Rose in a car seat. Luke and Megan were sharing a car with Tyler and Kendra. The only one missing was Tate with Lexi and Paisley. Gran was coming with him too.

The next few minutes were very loud as everyone bustled in. Avery was the center of attention, and she handled it well.

She was beside herself when we introduced Rose to her, but since she was sleeping, she stayed in the car seat.

Declan pulled the two of us into a corner right away.

"Declan, thank you so much for looking over my documents," Avery told him.

"My pleasure. I think we've got a case based on the stolen jewelry designs, but I don't want to get your hopes up yet. I'll keep you posted."

"Thanks," she said just as Kimberly joined us.

"Declan. Don't monopolize them. Avery, you've brought the jewelry?" Kimberly asked.

Avery nodded eagerly as we joined the group. "I left the bag near the hallway table. We can look over everything later."

"Hell yes."

"Guys, don't overwhelm her," I said, stepping next to my woman and putting an arm around her shoulders.

Kimberly waved her hand. "You've hogged her all to yourself for so long. Now it's our time with her. Shoo, shoo, move away."

I laughed but didn't budge.

"Hmm, this one's possessive, isn't he?" Reese said, looking at my hand on Avery's shoulder.

"Oh yeah," Avery confirmed. "Is it just him, or is it a family trait? I remember everyone being pretty intense."

"You remember right," Travis said. "Mom, what are we doing and where?"

"The table's set," she replied. "Everyone just go into the dining room."

"Damn. She's not making us work for once. That's something," Travis added.

Avery grinned. "I like your family. You've always had style."

I squeezed her shoulder. "Thank you for coming here with me today."

"I wouldn't miss a Maxwell Thanksgiving for the world. Is your grandmother coming too?"

"Yeah, she should be here any minute now, along with Tate, Paisley, and Lexi."

"I can't believe Tate has a daughter who's almost a teenager," Avery said as Liz and Declan approached.

"Hey, I'm Liz."

"You're the baker, right?" Avery asked.

Liz smiled brilliantly. "Yes, I am. I brought some goodies for later."

"Thank goodness. I brought pie, too, but I don't know if it's any good."

We all headed to the dining room, and I quirked a brow. They'd changed the table. This one was twice as long as the previous one.

"When did you get this?" I asked Dad.

"Three weeks ago. We realized we wouldn't have enough space at Thanksgiving otherwise."

"I insisted," Mom added, and Dad smiled.

"Happy wife, happy life. You'll do best to remember that."

"And we do," Travis said. "I live by that rule, Dad."

Avery grinned, looking around. It was like there wasn't any place in the world she'd rather be.

Tate, Lexi, Paisley, and Gran arrived a few minutes later.

"Beatrice, it's so good to see you again," Avery said.

"My girl, you've grown up beautifully. I was so happy when I found out you moved in with Sam. This lot was worried you two would do some... unorthodox bonding," she said with a careful look at Paisley, "but I was hoping that's exactly what would happen."

Avery blushed instantly. "You haven't changed at all. Still call everything like you see it."

"That's me," Gran agreed.

Lexi and Paisley started asking Avery about ordering jewelry the second after I introduced her. Lexi was far along her pregnancy, but I'd forgotten when her due date was.

I winked at Kimberly, who winked right back.

"Everyone, settle down," Mom ordered. "We'll have plenty of time for that later. It's time for the turkey."

Mom had gone all out. She'd already put the gravy and mashed potatoes on the table, along with stuffing and the cranberry sauce and a few other dishes. Some years she added corn, on others green beans. This year, it was the latter.

Dad went with her to the kitchen. They returned a few minutes later, carrying the world's largest turkey. We all started clapping.

"I've never seen such a big turkey," Avery commented.

I shook my head. "Neither have I. Then again, I've missed the last few Thanksgivings."

They put it at the head of the table, and Mom immediately started cutting it as we passed our plates around to have them filled with meat and fixings. Dad used to carve the bird, but Mom had wanted to learn how to do it one year and continued doing it from then on.

"I remember Lena's cooking. It was always delicious," Avery said.

"She's only gotten better over the years," Reese said.

Avery giggled. "I'm really feeling like we're on a scout outing or something, waiting to get food."

"We're not too far off," Luke said.

"Yeah, we're going to start behaving like our fifteen-year-old selves any second now, Avery," Travis added.

"I don't mind." She glanced at everyone. "Just so I'm up-to-date, Tate and Travis are the only ones with kids, right?"

"Yeah," Travis confirmed.

"Do you think the little nugget will wake up this evening?" Avery asked. Rose was fast asleep in the car seat.

"Honestly, probably not. She's usually in deep sleep at this time of the day," Bonnie said.

"Oh, that makes sense," Avery said, the disappointment

obvious in her voice. "I hope I get to spend time with her some-time soon."

Travis looked at me. "Sure, we could arrange something."

She wanted to spend time with my niece? Fuck me, this woman was adorable—and holding out on me. She'd never told me that.

Kimberly looked around the group, smilingly smugly.

"What?" I asked.

"Nothing. I'm just happy to finally see you again." She winked at Avery. "I can't wait to steal you away. You and I are going to be best friends. I have a good feeling about it."

"What a coincidence," Avery said. "So do I. It's a pity we never kept in touch."

"Well, I was very resentful of the fact that you'd broken Sam's heart. I was determined not to talk to you again."

Avery choked, and my jaw dropped.

"Kimberly," I said.

"Sorry, that was my—what age was I—seventeen-year-old judgment. I'm much more mature now," Kimberly said. "Of course, if anyone hurts any of my cousins, I might turn into a mama bear, but that's another conversation altogether."

"I quite like your mama bear personality," Kendra said. "It extends to us girls, too, by the way."

"Good to know," Avery said.

"How's your mom?" Reese asked.

"She's fine, thanks. She's healthy, thank goodness. She loves living in Florida. She's spending Thanksgiving with her friends."

"And your sister?"

"She's traveling with friends."

Once we were done with dinner, we all moved into the living room. Mom cut Avery's pie in the kitchen, and everyone was welcome to take a plate with a serving.

I was pleased that everyone was embracing Avery so openly,

not only my cousins and brothers, but also their wives and fiancées.

"Sam, you didn't update me. Did the board change their mind about sending you to the boonies for that clinic?" Kimberly asked.

I froze. Next to me, I felt Avery tense up. She looked at me. Mom gasped.

"What? You didn't tell me about that," Avery exclaimed.

Kimberly put her hand over her mouth. "Shit, Sam, you still didn't tell her? I didn't know it was still a secret."

"Kimberly, language," Gran said.

Kimberly cleared her throat. "Sorry, Gran. Sorry, Paisley."

"It's not a secret," I said slowly.

"Well, clearly Avery doesn't know, and I think part of the family… Okay, okay. I'm going to shut up now," Kimberly said.

She smiled apologetically at Avery, who sat uncharacteristically still.

"I'm not sure which of you is going to need the mama bear personality soon, but I'm here for both of you," Kimberly said. "I'm going to get seconds."

She walked to the kitchen just as Reese was heading in our direction. Kimberly caught her sister by the arm and whispered something in her ear. Reese's eyes widened, and she went toward Mom instead.

"I'm sorry you found out like this," I murmured to Avery. "Kimberly shouldn't have blurted it out."

"It's not her fault. She couldn't have known you didn't tell me." Her voice was strained.

I took her empty plate and put it on the coffee table next to mine.

"Want to take a walk in the backyard?" I asked.

"Sure."

We headed away from the living room, through the door that connected to the backyard. Outside, it was windy and far too chilly for my taste, but I wanted to have some alone time with my girl.

"Let me get your coat," I said.

"There's no need. Please, I just want to talk."

"Okay."

"How long have you known?"

"That's not important."

She looked up at me. Her eyes were furious. "Yes, it is."

"Robinson Matthew, the CEO, told me about six weeks ago."

"Weeks? You've known for *weeks*? So wait, all that time you were hinting at our future and you were secretly wondering how to tell me? Or were you going to tell me at all?"

"Avery." I made a move to touch her arms, but she took a step back. "Of course I meant to tell you. The thing is, I haven't accepted their deal."

Her shoulders dropped. "Why not?"

"Because it's in Maine, and it's not what I want."

"But that clinic is all you've been talking about."

"I want to open it in Chicago."

She swallowed hard, rubbing her arms with her palms.

"Are you sure you don't want your coat?"

"I'm fine."

"Avery, I'm not going to accept it."

"But it's your dream," she murmured.

"Yeah, but I'm flexible when it comes to that. My family is in Chicago. You're in Chicago."

"You were with Doctors Without Borders for years, Sam. You went all around the world, and your family was still in Chicago. What's changed?"

"You. Now I have you."

She shook her head. "No. This isn't right."

"What? What do you mean?"

"You shouldn't make a decision based on our relationship."

I stared at her. "Why the hell not?"

"Because things can happen. You can change your mind, or I can, or things fall apart, and then you'll regret that you stayed here."

"Way to be optimistic about the future." I was stunned.

In my mind, I'd kept rehearsing how I was going to break the news. The only variations were the words I would choose, but I had to admit I always thought her reaction would be to jump my bones and tell me how happy she was that I wasn't going anywhere.

"You don't mean that," I said.

She ran a hand through her hair. "It's just that I know how important dreams are and how crucial it is to go after them and fulfill them."

"So what you're saying is, if someone told you they would exponentially grow your business if you moved to London or something, you'd just pack up and leave."

"That's not what I'm saying at all."

"Sounds to me like you are. You're basically telling me not to choose you because you're not sure you want me for the long run."

She gasped. "Sam... I'm sorry. Is that what I said? It's not what I meant. Oh God. I'm so confused."

"Take all the time you need to think about what you really want to say. But for now, let's just go join everyone and enjoy the rest of the day. I don't want us to continue this conversation right now."

"I agree. We both need to think about... everything. Let's get back inside. I don't want anyone to worry."

"Sure."

My tone was clipped. The legendary Maxwell confidence led me to think that Avery saw the future just the way I did. But apparently she didn't.

I was starting to feel like an idiot.

AVERY

J couldn't sketch. I couldn't even work on organizational tasks. Quite honestly, I couldn't focus on anything at all. It had been two days since Thanksgiving. The rest of that evening went by awkwardly. Sam mostly spoke with Travis and Luke.

Kimberly, Reese, and the rest of the girls kept me occupied by giving me a million jewelry orders. Once we came home, we went straight to bed with no sexy times. The next morning, Sam went to the hospital before I woke up.

He hadn't come home since. First, I thought something must have switched up at the hospital and he had to take another shift, but now I was fairly certain he was avoiding me. I didn't like the way we'd left things, and he was clearly pissed off. To be honest, after he left, I rewound our conversation, and I got mad too. How did he turn everything against me? I'd never, ever told him I wouldn't choose him. Still, the truth was, deep down, I wanted *Sam* to choose *me*. I just didn't want him to know I wanted that because I was also afraid of him giving up his dream and resenting me for it.

I threw away the sketch I'd been working on—it looked like

crap. I had to come to terms with the fact that I wouldn't be able to do any creative work until Sam and I worked things out, or at least until he came home and I knew he was okay. I'd only texted him once, and he said he was sleeping in the on-call room. At least that was something; it meant he wasn't overworking himself.

While I made myself another coffee, I checked my phone. I didn't have a message from Sam, but I did have one from Kimberly.

Kimberly: Hey, your unwanted mama bear here. Do you need some company?

I replied quickly.

Avery: I'd love some. The loft is starting to feel quite lonely.

Kimberly: Yeah, I heard Sam is camping at the hospital. Want me to buy something for us to snack on?

Avery: Yes please.

Kimberly: Any favorites?

Avery: Whatever's bad for us.

That sounded good. I wasn't in the mood for alcohol. I mean, it was morning, for God's sake, but an extraordinary amount of carbs and sugar sounded right up my alley.

Since I knew Kimberly was coming, I went to the bathroom and made myself presentable.

I was wearing a pink summer dress, more of a Bohemian style. I loved lounging in them around the loft, even though it was cold as hell outside.

As I looked around, my heart felt like it was the size of a peanut. Seeing everything we'd done to this place in such a short time made me realize how much I wanted a future with him. I could almost see our mini-mes running around.

Oh God, I loved Sam so much, and our life together. These past few weeks, I'd convinced myself that we were a couple and this was a relationship. Now my heart was heavy at the thought that our paths could separate again. I couldn't even imagine us being apart.

Last time it had been different. I'd been in over my head with Mom's doctor appointments and the bills. I didn't even have time to mourn my breakup with Sam. I'd only woken up, as if from a haze, three years later. Back then, the wound was no longer fresh enough to grieve, but it had never healed properly.

Kimberly arrived faster than I thought she would. She smiled from ear to ear as I opened the door for her. My eyes bulged at the size of the box she was holding. It was from Liz's Bakery.

"How much stuff did you bring, exactly?"

"A lot. I told Liz what we're dealing with, and she said she knew exactly what to give us."

"Did Sam tell you something?"

"No, not at all, but just by the fact that he's sleeping at the hospital, and you couldn't reply fast enough that I should stop by, I think I'm on the right path, huh?"

I nodded.

We went to the kitchen island, and she opened the box.

"Wow. Everything looks delicious," I said.

"I agree."

"Well, let's see what we have here. What should we start with?"

"Can I make a suggestion?"

"Sure."

"Let's start with the bigger ones because the small ones are usually sweeter."

"We'll work up the ladder of sugar rush, so to speak," I said.

Kimberly snapped her fingers before pointing at me. "Exactly. You're good at this."

"I do my best." I took a huge cupcake and bit right into it. It had chocolate on the outside and a creamy liqueur frosting on the inside. "This is unexpected, and delicious," I muttered. "Kim, you're a godsend. I didn't even know I needed this."

She laughed softly. "Sam is the only one who calls me Kim."

"Really?"

She nodded. "Listen, I feel so bad for the way I blurted things out at Thanksgiving. I don't know what I was thinking. I thought he told you. I just figured it was up for discussion. I mean, in retrospect I should've known because no one brought it up. But I've been away for too long, and I seem to have forgotten some of the family dynamics. I'm going to get back in the saddle soon, though."

"Don't worry," I said. "These"—I pointed to the sweets—"more than make up for it."

"How's my jewelry coming along?" she asked, batting her eyelashes.

I sighed. "Not at all. I can't be creative right now."

Kimberly bit her lower lip. "I totally get that. When I'm consumed by relationship crap, I can only do mindless, robotic stuff."

"I promise I'll start working on them soon, though."

I'd shown everyone stones and designs and took their measurements. I'd agreed to make several designs for each, and they could choose their favorites. It was a far more sophisticated approach than I usually took with clients, but I wanted to go the extra mile for the family.

God, I wanted them to be my family so bad!

"I'm surprised Alana isn't here with you."

"She's on a business trip to Sydney," I said miserably. "Otherwise, she probably would've come in the evening to keep me company."

Kimberly gave me a sheepish smile. "If you want, we can go out and have some girly fun this evening."

"What if Sam comes home? I really want to talk to him."

"When my cousin eventually stumbles home, he'll probably crash and sleep for forty-eight hours straight. And if he doesn't, you probably shouldn't talk to him anyway because he's going to be exhausted and even more of a Maxwell male than usual."

"A what?" I understood the words, but they seemed to have some secret meaning.

"It's what Reese and I sometimes say about our cousins. It's a particular type of stubbornness that was only transmitted to the male side of our family. However, there's also a correlation: the more stubborn they are, the more they care about you."

"You think so?" I murmured.

"I'm positive about it."

"I just want him to come home."

Kimberly said, "He will, trust me. He so will. We have a plan."

"Who's 'we'? What plan?"

She smiled. "Just leave it to us."

* * *

Sam

THE BEDS in the on-call room were hands down the worst ones I'd ever slept in. Had they purposefully made them uncomfortable? Doctors needed their rest. I woke up with a stiff neck and a sore elbow, though that was probably not the bed's fault. I needed to go home.

The first two nights, I didn't even purposely stay here. Flu season was rampant, and three of my colleagues got sick. That meant I had to take over their shifts. In the morning, I was simply too exhausted to leave the hospital, so I fell asleep in the on-call room.

Tonight had been a conscious choice. I hadn't wanted to go home after two nights of disastrous sleep and face Avery. It was a well-known fact in the Maxwell clan that I didn't make the best decisions when I wasn't well rested.

There was a knock at the door. "Come in."

The door opened, and Tina poked her head in. "Hey, Sam,

Travis and Bonnie are here with little Rose. Thought you might want to say hi."

I immediately flipped into doctor mode. "Is it an emergency?"

"No, no. They're here for a checkup."

"Already?"

Tina frowned. "I just saw them come in, and I know how you like to see them during her checkups."

"I do." I felt a special bond with my niece. Maybe because I held her the day she was born. I'd always wanted children—but Avery's comments at Thanksgiving made me worry how committed she really was to us, our relationship. After Olivia, my ego was rawer than I thought.

I went up to pediatrics, massaging my stiff neck. Dr. Catson's exam room was just two corridors away from the elevator, but I managed to take the wrong one. Damn, I was definitely sleep-deprived. When I finally found it, I went in without knocking first. Travis and Bonnie were hovering over Rose. Dr. Catson was administering a shot, and little Rose was remarkably silent.

"Damn, she's not afraid at all," I said.

Travis looked at me. "How did you know we were here?"

"Tina told me. She saw you come in."

"She had to get a couple shots," Bonnie said, "and we hadn't been able to make an appointment, so we thought we'd stop by today."

I narrowed my eyes, looking from Travis to Bonnie. "When did you make that decision?"

"Yesterday."

The corners of my mouth were now twitching. This was an intervention.

Travis stared at me. "When we found out through the Maxwell-gossip-central-line that you were practically camping at the hospital…"

Dr. Catson looked at me, and I groaned. The last thing I

wanted was for my colleagues to know any of my business, but if anyone had to hear my drama, at least he was easygoing.

"I'm done here. My next patient isn't for another hour, so I'll leave the room for you all to chat."

"Sure." Bonnie kissed Rose's head.

Damn, she was cute. She hadn't even cried at the shots, which was rare. Then again, Dr. Catson had a way with kids. To my astonishment, my niece looked at me and extended a hand.

"I think that means she wants you to hold her," Bonnie said.

"But I haven't showered since yesterday, I think."

"Babies don't mind," Bonnie assured me.

I lifted my niece from Bonnie, and she immediately snatched my scrubs and planted her small lips right on my sternum. Then she turned around, just resting her cheek on it. "She's relaxed, and... oh, I can't believe it. She fell asleep."

"You're truly a baby whisperer. You should come visit us more often," Bonnie said.

She was right. The baby's breaths were even, though she sighed now and again. But babies sometimes did that in their sleep.

It was rare for anyone to actually fall asleep like this on someone who wasn't their parent. Maybe the bond I felt with her went both ways. My heart swelled with pride at the thought.

"You didn't have to come all the way here," I said softly, though Rose moved in my arms anyway. I made a sign to indicate I wasn't going to talk anymore because I didn't want to wake her up.

"Oh good, you're silent. That means we can talk," Travis said. I stared at him, cocking a brow, and then at Bonnie. "She doesn't wake up when other people talk. But if you speak, she might feel the vibrations in your body."

"Is this a trick?" I asked. The baby moved again, and I shut up.

"No, but it's working out wonderfully," Bonnie said. "We should remember it just in case anyone needs you quiet again."

Travis kissed her temple. "I like how you think, babe." He turned to me. "Sam, are you listening to me?"

"Yes." The baby didn't shift, so I took it as a good sign that one-word answers were okay.

"We all know how you can get when you haven't had your sleep," Travis began.

"I'm a doctor. I've been sleep-deprived since finishing med school."

"Shh," Bonnie said just as Rose started to wince.

I put a hand on the back of her head, caressing the top with my thumb, and her breathing eased again.

"Listen, we know you and Avery have a history, which includes her leaving after high school. And also that your ex was kind of a bitch." Though the way he said "bitch" was more like "beeotch," probably so Rose wouldn't understand, which was hilarious.

"She doesn't know what the word means," Bonnie said quickly when Travis cocked a brow at her. "The point is, we know you weren't looking for a relationship when Avery came back in your life."

"Listen to me, man. I've known Avery for as long as you have. Obviously, as a twenty-year-old, I couldn't assess the situation. But as an adult, my guess is that back then, she didn't want to stand in the way of your career, and then in some twisted way, now it's happening all over again," Travis continued.

"I hear you, bro, but that doesn't make sense. She's not stopping me from doing anything. I don't want to move to Maine. I want to stay here with her in Chicago."

"Right, so your choice is stopping you from going to Maine to build the clinic, and she thinks you're doing that because of her," Travis said.

Could this be any more confusing?

"But I told her I am choosing Chicago because of her. I choose her."

"I'm impressed," Travis said. "But I think Avery's unsure." He looked at his wife. "I don't know. Babe? Help me out here."

"Yeah, those were all the right words, Sam. And look, Rose isn't even waking up, so she approves of them too," Bonnie said. "But sometimes it takes more than words. Something like a romantic gesture."

"I think Tate could give you some insights. Gran probably could too," Travis said.

Bonnie chuckled. "Must everything be a Maxwell group effort?"

"No, not everything," he replied, wiggling his eyebrows.

"But they usually are awesome," I agreed.

After they were left, I changed and did the same. Travis was right. I'd told Avery what I wanted. Now I needed to prove it to her.

26

AVERY

*K*imberly and I ate our combined weight in sweets. Somehow, the sugar rush also brought on a bout of creativity. Now I was suddenly sketching. Kimberly was pacing around as we talked about everything and nothing. She was mostly bashing her last boyfriend, who'd also happened to be her boss back in Paris. In between, she kept asking me stuff about Chicago, which I thought was a bit weird. I mean, she'd been away for a few years, but surely she knew the city better than I did. I'd been gone since graduating high school.

"So if there's one thing you would absolutely love to do tonight, what would it be?" she asked all of a sudden while I finalized the clasp.

"I'd love to go on a boat out on the lake. I've never been," I said, turning around the sketch for her to see.

A huge smile lit up her face, and she stood straighter. That was a very enthusiastic reaction to my sketch. I approved.

"I love that!" she exclaimed. "Oh, you've got such a way with jewelry. I like the shape of the pendant." I'd drawn in a straight column but added a spiral on it so it gave the appearance of a fluid image. "And boats, huh? That's interesting to know."

I frowned. "Is it really?"

She nodded. "Oh yeah. Let me just send this text message."

"You want to share the sketch with Reese?"

Kimberly's eyes widened. "Sure," she said in a tone that told me that wasn't at all what she was doing. But she snapped a picture of the sketch before sending the message. Still smiling, she came and sat on the couch next to me, stretching out her hand. I gave her the drawing, and she inspected it carefully.

"You know, I heard from Sam that you're missing your old business, but I have to say, I think you're meant to do what you're doing."

"Oh, I think so too," I said. "I never realized how much heart I can put into this, especially the custom orders. I've got a few more ideas just for you. Let me get to work."

"Please do."

I was so lost in my sketching that I didn't even realize my phone was beeping twenty minutes later.

"Earth to Avery," Kimberly said, sounding overly enthusiastic. "The phone."

"Oh yeah, right." I'd been sitting on it. As I grabbed it from under my ass, I nearly dropped it on the floor. "I've got a message from Sam."

"I know."

"You do?"

Kimberly blushed. "I mean, I assumed it would be from him."

Sam: Babe, I'm coming home. I'm whisking you away and making up for the past few days.

I squealed, turning it around so Kimberly could see.

She nodded her approval. "Short and sweet. Let's get you ready. You need a gorgeous dress."

I was about to reply to Sam when her words registered. I looked up at her. "What are you talking about? I don't even know where I'm going."

The corners of her mouth tipped up. "I do."

"Wait, what? What is happening right now?"

"You're in the midst of a Maxwell… Hmm, what shall we call it? Intervention? Tornado? Whatever, girl. Just go with it. Trust me."

"I haven't finished your sketch."

She smiled sweetly. "You can do it another time. He didn't say when he's coming, huh?"

"No, I was about to text him and ask."

"Yeah, you do that."

Avery: What do you mean, whisking me away? When should I be ready? And why does Kimberly know?

Sam: She told you she knows? I'm not telling Kimberly a thing ever again. I'll be home in about an hour.

Avery: What makes you so sure I want to go with you? I mean, you've been gone for two days.

Sam: I know, babe. And I plan to make up for every moment I missed, I promise.

I was too excited to play coy, and my stomach was somersaulting. I had a gazillion butterflies in it.

I turned to Kimberly. "Okay, let's go to my room, and I'll show you all my clothes."

Forty minutes later, I looked like a doll. I was wearing a mid-calf red velvet dress. I'd forgotten I even owned it, but Kimberly found it at the back of my closet. She'd done my hair in an interesting style off to the side. The top part was a braid, but it was loose over my shoulder.

"Is this a French look?" I asked, glancing in the mirror and twirling around. "I feel French."

"Let's call it a fusion look. I wouldn't say my hairdos are French, but they're inspired by them."

After Kimberly and I went back in the living room, she checked her phone. "Time for me to disappear."

"Why?" I asked.

"I don't want to be a cockblocker, to quote Travis."

"Well, I mean, you know, I don't think we'll..." I stammered. "Travis? What does he know?" Now I was all confused.

She grinned. "Never mind. Whatever you do or don't do is between the two of you. I've done my part. Just don't cry or you'll ruin your makeup."

She'd taken her sweet time with that. She blew me an air kiss before disappearing out the door.

I felt like everything was happening too fast for me to process. Had she come here today specifically for this? That couldn't be. Then again, the Maxwell family group worked in mysterious ways. They'd been like this even when we were kids.

Now that I was alone in the enormous loft, I started to get nervous again. What if Sam reiterated that he was staying here for me? How could I express that what I wanted was for him to be happy without him getting the wrong idea again? The butterflies in my belly turned to stone.

A knock at the door took me out of my thoughts, and I went straight toward it. It opened before I got there, and Sam was standing in the doorway, grinning from ear to ear.

"Why did you knock?" I asked as he closed the door behind him.

"I wanted to give you a heads-up."

He was wearing a suit. It was dark blue with a white shirt underneath, and it fit him perfectly.

"Where did you get that suit? All your clothes are here."

"Yeah, but there are plenty of shops in the city, and shopping was faster."

He stepped over to me, taking my hands. I felt warm all of a sudden. He kissed my right hand and then my left one.

"Avery, I'm sorry about the past few days. There have been a lot of flu cases at the hospital, and I had to move a few shifts. And I won't lie. I wasn't sure where to pick up our conversation."

"And now you are?" I asked. My heart was in my throat.

"Hell yes, babe. I know where to start. I love you. I love you

211

with my whole heart, and I can't believe I'm lucky enough to have you."

Yep, I'd started to melt. "I love you too. So much," I murmured.

He kissed my right hand again, raining kisses up my arm until he reached the inside of my elbow. My skin turned to goose bumps.

He straightened, looking at me with a serious expression. "Come on. We need to go."

"Now?" I practically screamed. I was looking forward to some of that activity Kimberly didn't want to block.

He touched my cheek. "Yeah, we're on a schedule, but I promise it'll be worth it."

"You've already promised that, like, three times tonight."

"Trust me, babe."

He took my coat from the hanger, holding it out for me, and I put it on, tying it around my waist. "Where are we going?"

"You'll see. Kimberly didn't spoil that too?" he asked sharply.

"No, she didn't."

"Good, because I want it to be a surprise."

* * *

"WHAT ARE WE DOING HERE?" I asked when we stepped out of the Uber half an hour later. We were on the shore of the lake. When I'd seen the address on the Uber's GPS, I thought we might go to dinner somewhere on the harbor, but now I wasn't so sure. There weren't any fancy restaurants in the vicinity.

Sam caught my eye and smiled. "I heard you've always wanted to go on a romantic boat ride. I thought this might be the time for it."

"Oh my God. I'd love to. Kimberly did a fabulous job today, didn't she?"

"She did." Taking my right hand, he kissed the back of it,

bringing me closer to him. "I've been a fool these past few days, Avery, and I'm very sorry for that."

"I was just concerned about you. I didn't want you to miss out on an opportunity in Maine because of me."

"Babe, don't even think that." He pressed his lips to my cheek, giving me a chaste kiss before saying, "Come on. Let's go get on board."

"Okay." I was giddy with excitement.

He led me to something that looked more like a yacht than a boat. It had a large outdoor deck, but we went directly inside. Once we were indoors, I realized no one else was there, and that someone must have prepared it for us, because it was warm and cozy. There were three seats in the front, then a dining table and a couch in the back.

"Do you know how to drive this?"

"Yeah. All of us Maxwell kids received a safety course and got our license as a graduation gift."

"Nice thinking from your parents."

"They figured since Lake Michigan is at our doorstep, we should make the most of it. Are you comfortable?" Sam asked as we sat down in front.

"Yes, this is wonderful Sam. Are we going somewhere special?"

"Not really. I thought we'd go out until we don't see the shore-line, and then we can decide from there."

"That is a great plan." I couldn't help but look around as the boat sped up and the city blurred in the distance. It was already dark outside, so once the light went behind us, I couldn't see anything at all around us.

I tugged at his sleeve and said, "Let's stop here."

He nodded, flashing me that charming smile I loved so much. He went to the dashboard, pressing a few buttons. The boat stopped a few seconds later.

"It feels like we're out in the middle of the ocean, doesn't it?" I asked.

"Yeah, it kind of does. You look so elegant."

"So do you."

Taking my hand, he led me toward the couch in the back, and we both sat down. He cleared his throat.

I kept glancing around. "Is dinner going to pop out of nowhere?"

"No, that's waiting for us back at home. Avery, I wanted to bring you here because I wanted tonight to be special. I want to make you a few promises, and this seemed fitting."

"Besides, I can't run away, can I?"

We both start laughing.

"That crossed my mind," Sam said.

"Genius as always," I replied.

He caressed the back of my hand with his thumb and then tugged at my hand, pointing at his lap. I immediately rose from the bench, but instead of sitting like a lady would on his lap, I picked up the hem of my dress and straddled him.

He grinned. "That's my woman."

"This is more comfortable," I said.

27

AVERY

"Avery." His voice sounded serious. My stomach constricted. "When you told me I shouldn't base this decision on you, I had a flashback to all those years ago when you basically told me you were leaving town and leaving me behind."

"Oh, Sam. I'm so sorry."

"No. That was on me, not on you. You simply told me how you felt, and I jumped to conclusions based on a decision we made when we were much younger and didn't know any better. But now we do. I do. You're my whole life, Avery, and we've lost many years being apart, but I don't care. We can't make them up, and we have so many more before us. All I want to know is if you want to experience them with me, next to me."

"Yes, I do," I murmured. "It's all I ever wanted. I was thinking that even if I opened a physical store, I could probably do that in Maine or whatever."

"No, babe. We're not going anywhere."

"Sam."

"I've planned everything out."

"You have?"

"Yeah. I think all of this has been a long time coming, but the pieces just needed to fall into place."

"Meaning?" I ask.

"I needed to meet you again."

"Sam, the things you say."

He skimmed his hands up my thighs, and my skin instantly became sensitive. Heat gathered between my legs. Damn, I was already losing my composure. Actually, I probably started losing it when I saw him come up to me in the suit because he looked so damn sexy.

"I think we needed the time apart to get to this place in our lives. Now we're both ready."

"I love you, Sam."

"Not more than I do. I've never been happier than I have these past few months we've spent together as roommates."

"We were pretty insane to think we could pull it off, huh? Just living next to each other, like we actually thought it would be platonic."

"Yeah. Got to give it to my family again. They were right. Virtually none of them thought we could do that."

I started laughing so hard, my shoulders were shaking. "That does sound like your family."

"I want to give you something." He reached inside his pocket, taking out a folded sheet of paper.

Frowning, I opened it up. "Oh my God, tickets to Paris!"

"Hell yes, baby."

"When are we going?"

"They're open-ended. We can decide on that later."

"I can't believe it. We're going to Paris. I've always wanted to."

"I know, babe. I know."

I put them down on the coffee table so I could give him a huge smooch.

"Oh, Sam. You're so romantic," I whispered.

"Glad you think so, babe. I'm not even done yet."

"Oh, there's more? You think you haven't made me swoon enough?"

"Someone told me nothing is ever enough."

I grinned. "I agree with whoever gave you that advice. Does it happen to be a Maxwell?"

"Obviously, considering there are so many of us. I don't even bother asking anyone else for advice."

I chuckled. "Good for you."

"I love you, Avery, with my whole heart, with everything I have. This doesn't mean I will give up on my dream."

He cupped the side of my face with one palm and ran the fingers of his other hand down my neck. "See, one thing I've learned from you is that you can make your dream come true anywhere. Sometimes coming back to your hometown, to the place where your roots are, is the best thing that can happen to you."

"And Chicago is your hometown," I confirm.

"No, babe, you are. My brothers suggested a while ago that I could reach out to them for management advice if I wanted to open the pro bono clinic independent of the hospital. And that's what I'll do. I'm a doctor, but I'm also a Maxwell. And I'm proud of it. You're my home, Avery. I want to be exactly where you are, babe. We can build our life together, help each other succeed in our dreams, console each other when the day goes to shit."

"As long as it's not with cocktails that I make, it's all good," I whispered.

God, he was saying such nice things, and I believed him 100 percent. We could do this. I didn't know why I doubted it before. It was probably because that little girl I used to be who was afraid her shitty life would run him off was still inside me somewhere. But I chose to be strong every single day.

He kissed me slowly, but it was so damn hot that I felt as if my clothes were going to catch fire soon, and my body, for sure. I felt that kiss in every cell. God, I'd missed him so much these past few days. I was exhausted from all the anguish of thinking I might lose him for good and now from the relief of knowing that not only did he love me, but he wanted to stay here with me.

He deepened the kiss, and I felt one of his hands tug at my spaghetti strap. Heat coursed through me as I realized how much he wanted me.

Groaning, he lifted us both to our feet. Taking a step back, he looked at me. Keeping my balance wasn't terribly easy, since the boat moved with the motion of the lake.

He held up a finger, indicating for me to twirl, and I did just that. Then he wrapped his arms around my waist from behind, kissing under the lobe of my ear.

"You're so damn beautiful," he murmured.

I had goose bumps everywhere. He could tell me that a million times, and every time I'd have the same reaction.

"I love you," I whispered.

"And I love you, babe."

He loosened his grip on me just for a second, and I saw my opportunity to tease him.

"Show me, then." I half walked, half strutted toward the dining table, trying to be extra sexy.

He was right behind me in a second.

"Don't move," he said.

"You're starting with the orders already."

He brought an arm around my waist and cupped my center over the dress. I'd soaked my panties through. "Mmm," he said, "and you are enjoying it."

"Oh God, yes."

I didn't want to hide how much I wanted him all the time. How much my body simply longed for him.

He rubbed me over the fabric with one finger and then two. I gasped, buckling forward.

"Sam," I murmured, and then he yanked down my dress. I was wearing garters, and he had easy access to my panties.

He immediately slid a hand inside them. He undid my bra with the other one, cupping my breast and kneading my nipple.

On instinct, I rolled my hips, rubbing against him. Even through his pants, I could feel how turned on he was. His touch on my bare skin was exquisite. I tried to fumble with my fingers behind my back and finally succeeded in opening the button and lowering his zipper.

I wrapped one hand around his cock, squeezing.

"Fuck," he exclaimed in my ear. That word alone sent fire raging through me.

"Sam, I need you," I murmured.

"You'll have me, babe. That's a promise."

"I need you right now."

"That's not going to happen. You look so gorgeous, and I plan to explore you until you beg for me."

"Oh." My voice trembled. My entire body did. I loved this side of him.

Promptly, he took his hand away from my panties. I gasped, feeling suddenly cold. There was a growing pit inside me that I needed him to fill.

He turned me around slowly. Lowering himself, he clamped his mouth around one of my nipples. He had both hands free right now and used them to undo the garters from the ties before returning to my pussy.

If I thought I couldn't get even more turned on, I was wrong. The way his fingers played me was insane. A wave of pleasure exploded through me. It was like a small orgasm, but I knew it wasn't the real deal. Far from satisfying me, it only made me hungrier for him.

"Sam!" My voice broke. "Please."

He looked up at me, and I felt him smile wickedly against my breast before he took his mouth away. I didn't even have time to protest before he led me to the couch.

"Sit down," he instructed the second the back of my calves touched the edge.

I immediately sat on the soft leather. My knees were still bent over the edge of the couch. I thought he was going to take down my panties. Instead, he pushed the fabric exactly where it covered my center to one side and then pressed his tongue against my flesh. I felt like I was going to break out of my skin.

"Sam. God, Sam, please."

Then he took my panties down slowly, torturing me, before he buried his face between my legs.

My senses overwhelmed me instantly. My vision blurred at first, and then it turned completely dark. My orgasm simply exploded inside me the second I felt his lips on my clit. The after-shocks racked my whole body. I moved wildly on the couch, no longer in control of my muscles. I bent my right leg, pushing my buttocks off the leather. I cried out so loud that I was almost ashamed, then remembered we were in the middle of the lake.

"Oh God, you sound so damn delicious."

I heard his voice as if from a distance.

He kissed up my body, but he took his sweet time, starting at my ankles. I wasn't even sure if I was recovering from my orgasm or was simply getting turned on again. Maybe a bit of both. I felt every kiss intensely, as if my skin was simply too sensitive for his lips and his callused hands. When he kissed my inner thigh, I thought he was going to put his mouth on my center again, but he moved even farther until he trailed up my neck and then went to my ear.

"I want to make you mine like this every single day."

"Promise," I whispered.

"I fucking promise, babe."

He kissed down my torso, but I wasn't going to let him get away with torturing me for too long. I could reach his cock from this position, and that was exactly what I did. I pumped it up and down, pressing my thumb across the crown.

"Jesus," he exclaimed, dropping his head back and groaning. He leaned over and kissed my neck once more. I braced myself, digging my fingers into the leather. I was still so sensitive and tight from my last orgasm that I released a deep, guttural sound when he slowly pushed inside me. I pulsed around him.

"Oh God, this feels good. This is so good."

I almost came apart from the sensation of having all of him inside me. I could barely catch my breath. I balled my hands into fists, needing to brace myself; I knew this orgasm would simply tear me apart.

He pulled back and thrust inside harder. The slapping sounds of our bodies filled my mind, intensifying my emotions.

"Oh," I moaned. My voice was shaky, and so was my body.

I braced myself, and then I took one hand away, needing to touch him. I reached the side of his thigh. It was clenched from the effort he was making as he thrust and thrust inside me, fast and deep. Nothing could ever feel more perfect than this… except his hand on my clit. When I felt the brush of his fingers, my thighs almost gave in.

I was completely lost in Sam. I wasn't sure if the grunts were truly mine or his, or perhaps they belonged to both of us. It was pure sensation. I wasn't even aware of my body anymore, just of the immense pleasure this man was giving me.

I exploded with a muffled cry, burying my face in the armrest. My entire body went from being strung tight and on edge to feeling like I was floating. I heard Sam cry out my name. I loved that sound so much.

I loved him.

28

AVERY

TWO WEEKS LATER

"*B*abe, you've already snapped a picture of the Eiffel Tower."

"Make that fifty," Kimberly exclaimed.

I scoffed. "Excuse me. It's the first time I've been here, and I love it."

Sam and Kimberly exchanged a glance and laughed. I couldn't even feel embarrassed. I was too excited. The three of us came to Paris together. I'd insisted Kimberly come with us—she was practically a local, and she knew the best spots and secret gems.

We flew via London because Beatrice wanted to visit her son. I was so happy she'd made amends with Kimberly's dad. I remembered the sadness in her eyes back when I was a teenager whenever she spoke about him, and I was more than happy that their relationship had improved.

Sam, Kimberly, and I even met her gentleman friend. I, for one, really liked him, and so did Kimberly. Sam was still reserving judgment.

"This is even more beautiful than in pictures," I said with wonder. I was happy to be here, strolling the large boulevards and eating the most delicious sweets. I must have eaten six éclairs in the time we'd been here, and I was buying chocolate almost every day, as well as a ton of other goodies. We were here for a week, and it seemed far too short.

"Why did you leave the city?" I asked Kimberly.

She shrugged. "It was just time to come home."

Ah yes, the Maxwells and their home base. I totally knew what she meant. Her whole family was there. Well, except for her dad. Still, knowing the family, I was surprised any of them had moved away at all.

"Sam, what are we doing next?" I asked.

"I actually have to go meet a friend. I think you two will be able to find your way around." Kimberly winked at Sam.

He nodded. "Yes, we will. Thanks for all the tips, cousin."

"Anytime. You can call me if you get lost or something."

"Sure."

"Are you meeting us for dinner?" I asked.

She gave me an enigmatic smile. "We'll see."

Hmm. Okay, maybe she had other plans. I didn't want to interfere. She really did have amazing tips. I wanted to do all sorts of tourist stuff, but she'd also given us plenty of suggestions for things locals liked.

"What are we doing next?" I asked Sam.

"What do you have on that huge list of yours?"

"The entire city, so let's prioritize and see what's around here."

"Great idea."

The Garden of the Eiffel Tower was amazing. Everywhere I looked there were trees. They were leafless now, but I imagined that in warmer months, it was a sea of green. There were a lot of tourists, but it was still spacious enough that it didn't feel crowded at all. We'd already checked some of the stuff off that was on my list. We'd been to the Louvre, spent one day at Versailles, and went up the million steps or so to Sacré Coeur, where the view of the city was absolutely stunning. We'd also seen the Arc de Triomphe, of course.

My favorites so far were the Champs-Élysées and the Eiffel Tower. They were stunning up close, but I preferred a long-distance view to take in all of their majesty. It was also better for photos, which I posted on social media so my mom and sister could follow our trip.

"By the way, you know we're passing the stand Kimberly mentioned makes the best *choux à la crème* in the city?" Sam asked.

"Oooooh. That's been at the very top of my list."

"I know. You circled it in pink and then in blue."

I smiled sheepishly. "I didn't want to miss it. When you look at the list, it doesn't automatically jump out at you. It's easy to get distracted by things like the *Mona Lisa*."

"Interesting that *choux à la crème* is as important as the *Mona Lisa*."

"Don't make fun of me. I want to taste everything Paris has to offer so I don't forget it."

"I know you won't, babe. Besides, we can come back any time you want."

"Maybe. The first time is special, you know?"

I was already salivating from the wafts of sugar and vanilla in the air. There was a huge line in front of the stand. My stomach rumbled as we took our spot. We waited for twenty minutes, but it was completely worth it. The treat was the equivalent of cream puffs back home, only these were amazing.

"Oh my God. This is the best thing I've ever eaten," I exclaimed after the first one. We ate directly from the paper plate.

"I'll be damned. They are good," Sam exclaimed.

I ate the next two slowly, and Sam did the same. Then he took my hand in his, kissing it. I loved it when he did that, and I was so glad we were sharing this experience of Paris together.

"Are you done with these sweets?" he asked.

"Yep, not even one left."

"Do you want to get more?"

"No, I'm good."

"How are you feeling?"

"The happiest I've ever been."

He grinned. "Good. It increases my odds."

"Your odds?" I asked, confused.

The next thing I knew, he'd lowered himself to the ground. Wait, he wasn't bending or crouching. He was getting down on one knee.

"Oh, Sam," I exclaimed, realizing what was happening. My face exploded in a smile before I even saw him reach into his pocket. He took out a very small sachet.

"I wanted a box, but you would've seen it in my pocket and gotten suspicious."

"I would," I admitted.

He took the ring from the sachet, holding it so I could see it.

I gasped. "Sam! I remember this ring."

"I know. So do I."

A lifetime ago, I'd told him that if I ever got engaged—yeah, I wasn't very subtle in high school—I would love to get the Tiffany Setting ring.

It was absolutely beautiful. The diamond was round, set in a platinum band.

"Avery, I love you with my whole heart, with everything I have. I am so happy our paths crossed again." His voice sounded raspy. "I was lucky to have met you in high school, and I can't believe I've been lucky enough to meet you again. I love you, and I want to love you every day for the rest of our lives. To wake up and know you're mine. I promise to make you happy to the best of my abilities every single day."

"Oh, Sam." I bounced up and down from my toes to my heels. "I love you. And you do. You already make me so happy. I mean, you just waited in line for twenty minutes even though you didn't want sweets. That's proof that you're the perfect man for me."

He winked. "As I said, I knew it would increase my odds."

"You waited for a sugar rush. Clever. As if I was going to say no."

"Wasn't going to take any chances with you."

I couldn't believe it. He'd timed all this. Not only had he brought me to Paris, but he'd waited until the end of the tour to see which of my places was the favorite to propose. Of course, the sweets were the cherry on the top.

"I'm going to make you so happy," I promised him.

"Avery, will you be my wife for better or worse, for our whole lives?"

"Yes, I will," I said.

As if from a distance, I heard several people cheer and realized we had an audience of sorts. Some were taking pictures of us. Sam laughed as we looked around.

Rising to his feet, he put on my ring, which fit perfectly, and then lifted me slightly in his arms. I put my hands on his shoulders, leaning in for a kiss. It was chaste, but from the press of his lips against mine, I knew he could barely wait for us to be alone.

"We got great pictures of you," someone said in an American accent.

Sam and I smiled at the same time before pulling apart.

"Thank you. That's great. We'll always have this memory." I didn't have the heart to tell this well-meaning stranger that she interrupted our magnificent moment. But I could let it slide because, as Sam predicted, I was over the moon.

I'm going to be Mrs. Sam Maxwell.

While the lady and Sam exchanged numbers, I couldn't help but admire my ring. Afterward, the crowd that had formed around us dispersed, and Sam burst out laughing.

"Well, we'll certainly remember that. Look, she sent me the pictures already."

"It was worth being interrupted because otherwise we wouldn't have gotten them," I said. "Once we get back home, I'll tell my mom and sister and send them the pictures. They'll be thrilled to see how romantic you are."

He nodded. "True. That's one thing I didn't plan for. I'm half impressed Kimberly didn't jump out from behind the bush or something."

"She planned this moment with you?"

"No. She said to play it by ear and take my cues from what seemed to bring you the most joy."

"I love Kimberly to bits," I exclaimed.

"Yeah, it was a great idea," he murmured, turning around to face me, touching my cheek. "Except for one thing."

"What?"

"We're not anywhere close to our hotel."

I felt my cheeks turn hot. "Hey, we still have some things on the list."

His eyes darkened. "I see. So your *list* ranks above sex with me?"

I cleared my throat. "I wouldn't say that. But we *are* in Paris, you know? We should take advantage. And I can take advantage of you all you like once we're back home."

"Nothing against Paris, but I can't wait to go back home," he said a little glumly.

I laughed, taking his hand and pulling him toward the Eiffel Tower. "Come on, sexy fiancé. The quicker we get through my list, the quicker we'll get back to the room."

He grinned. "That's more like it."

EPILOGUE

Christmas Day

*C*hristmas Day was hands down my favorite day of the year, and we were spending it at Sam's parents' house. I felt like a child, surrounded by all the decorations. His mom went all out. She had four Christmas trees in the huge living room. I was taking mental notes for next year. I only had one lonely tree at the loft, and I could do so much better.

The house smelled spectacular. There were garlands with dried slices of orange hanging all around; every room had a delicious natural smell. Kimberly also made mulled wine, and I couldn't wait to taste it.

Cooking for Christmas in the Maxwell household was a whole-family affair. There were far too many of us to be in the kitchen at the same time, but Lena had worked out a shift system, so to speak. Everyone had something to do, but we all had breaks in between to enjoy ourselves.

"Mom, you're getting better and better at organizing us," Sam said. The two of us were currently at our stations at the kitchen island, chopping the garnish for the main course.

That was another thing Lena had insisted on, and it was genius. We wouldn't serve all the courses at once; instead, we'd spread them throughout the day so there was no pressure to get all the food ready at one time. She'd made roast beef with mashed potatoes for the main meal. Sam and I were making a salad.

"At first, I thought about preparing everything as I had for Thanksgiving and precook most of the food. But I wasn't too happy with how everything turned out. Some things weren't hot enough, and, well, I thought I could do better," she replied.

"It was perfect," I assured her.

Lena smiled at me. "You're a darling to say that."

"Mom is a perfectionist. She always tries to optimize everything." Sam winked at her.

As soon as we were done with the garnish, Lena instructed us to take it to the table. That was another golden rule: as soon as something's done, put it on a table immediately.

It was almost dinnertime now. We'd had a round of appetizers at lunch and a second round two hours ago. No one was starving, because there were cookies and snacks all around the living room. As soon as I put down the garnish with cilantro, I hurried to Bonnie, who grinned, kissing Rose's head.

"You're here for another cuddle session?" she asked.

I nodded eagerly, holding my hands out. As soon as she transferred her into my arms, I brought her to my chest. She put her little arms around my neck, kissing my cheek.

"Oh my God, she knows how to do that now," I said, feeling like my heart was about to explode. She was currently my favorite Maxwell right after Sam. She was so cute and smelled like sugar. I didn't have much experience with babies, but I had fallen head over heels for Rose. I'd found an excuse or five to go to Bonnie's place a couple times a week. Most of those excuses included jewelry, but everyone was happy. Bonnie was getting jewelry, and I was getting cuddle time. It was a win-win. But today I had to compete for my snuggles because everyone wanted to hold her whenever they weren't on shift. Kimberly and Reese in particular seemed to fight me for every minute.

I was waiting for one of them to pop up behind me and tell me it was their turn, but this time Lena herself interrupted, announcing that a new course was ready. I loved their tradition of celebrating Christmas all day long.

I was going to do something similar at the loft next year. I'd already decided on that. It was big enough to host all of the Maxwells, plus my mom and Jamie. I really hoped they were going to join us next year.

Lena invited them this year, but Mom had already agreed to go on a cruise with some of her friends, and she didn't want to cancel. I think if I pestered her some more, she might have, but I didn't want her to come out of guilt. I was happy she was healthy and enjoying life. Jamie already had plans with her friends. She told me she was seeing a new guy and things were progressing quickly. I was so happy for her.

"What are you thinking about?" Sam asked as he came up to me. He kissed the baby's hand, and my heart sighed.

"That we could host Christmas next year."

His eyes lit up. "I'm all for it, babe, but… maybe we can ask everyone to bring a dish."

"And if I make a system similar to your mom's, I won't even have to subject everyone to my cooking."

He nodded somberly. "Yeah. I would talk to Mom about keeping you under strict supervision."

I elbowed him lightly. "Hey. I'm trying to get better at cooking."

"Who knows? We might even move out of the loft by next year," he said.

We kept thinking about it, but honestly, at this point it just wasn't a priority. He was busy, still working at the hospital while supervising the process of starting his clinic.

I was a busy bee too. My custom-made jewelry business was

going well. A couple weeks ago, Declan and Sam worked their Maxwell magic, as I liked to call it. It turned out Declan was right. I could sue Sophia for stealing my designs—and in proving she had ill intent, he recouped every cent she stole too.

Being able to pay all my debt was a huge relief. I could now focus on the future without feeling the past dragging me down. I was immensely grateful to both Declan and Sam.

"Come on. Give her back to me so you can eat," Bonnie told me.

"I could keep her, you know, while you eat first," I suggested, not ready to part with my darling girl yet.

"No, she's very fussy at the table, but I know just what she needs," Bonnie said, so I reluctantly gave back the baby.

Sam put an arm around my shoulders and brushed his lips against my temple. "You're adorable," he murmured.

I blushed and pulled back a notch, looking up at him and grinning. "She just captured me. She's so cute and has some Maxwell charm, even though she's tiny. Although, to be fair, that might just be baby charm."

We all sat around the huge table. Sam and I were opposite Beatrice, who was looking at us with warm eyes. "I'm so glad you're here with us, Avery," she said unexpectedly.

"I'm happy, too, Beatrice."

She looked at Sam, then at Travis, who was sitting next to me. "And I'm glad my advice is making the rounds in the family. I heard about the boat trip."

Don't blush, Avery. Don't blush. She doesn't know the details, just that we went on a boat trip.

"Oh?" I asked, hoping she couldn't tell my face was on fire.

"Gran is the one who taught us the art of the grand gesture," Tate explained.

"Oh!" I had a whole new appreciation for Beatrice. I looked around at the girls, who smiled, looking warmly at their guys.

"I think I speak for all the women here when I say we owe you a big thanks, Beatrice," I said.

"My pleasure. That's the one good thing about being old as dirt: I know all the tricks in the book, and I don't mind sharing them. And I'm happy my grandkids are fast learners and that they listen to their old gran."

Sam kissed my hand. "Well, I'm thankful to the whole family this year. But most of all for reconnecting with Avery."

"See, he's got his girl, and now it's like we're second-rate citizens," Luke muttered for the whole table to hear him.

I started laughing along with everyone else. I was blushing even more than before.

"Don't be a buffoon, Luke," Sam said.

"Impossible," Declan said. "That's just who he is."

"Someone needs to be the yin to your yang, brother," Luke said, patting Declan on the shoulder. "Otherwise, you'd bring down the whole mood with your sunny personality."

Sam looked at Beatrice, then at me and said, "Gran, you were right all those years ago when you told me to go chase after her. But I'm also happy I didn't take your advice."

Beatrice smiled. "Hindsight is twenty-twenty. I'm happy the two of you met again at the right time."

That was exactly how I felt. Also, Beatrice had told him to chase after me? I loved her even more than before, and I hand't thought that was possible.

"I'm also grateful to all of you for the help you're providing with the Maxwell Clinic," Sam announced.

"Hey, we're happy you're finally acknowledging you're a Maxwell," Travis said lazily, taking the baby from Bonnie, who was now trying to eat her meal.

That was true. For as long as I'd known Sam, he'd seemed determined to prove to everyone that he could do things on his own. I was also happy that he was embracing his legacy and building on it.

"Honey, we're so thrilled to have you back in Chicago," Lena said. "And to help out with the clinic."

Getting the clinic up and running was a family effort. All the brothers, Reese and Kimberly, and Lena and Emmett were involved.

"I'm very glad for that. If someone told me last year that this Christmas would be so full of surprises, I wouldn't have believed it," Sam said.

"I have another one," Beatrice added.

I swear to God, the whole table went scary still. No one was even chewing. I wondered if we were all holding our breath.

"Don't be so tense," she said, sounding way too innocent. "Remember I told you about that gentleman I was seeing?"

"Yes," everyone chorused.

"Well, Sam, Kimberly, and Avery already met him. I'd like for the rest of you to meet him too. I told him he could drop by tomorrow. You're all invited to my house."

Everyone seemed to start talking at the same time as they asked her more about him and what she had planned. Beatrice was fielding questions left and right.

Once everyone agreed to go to her house the next day, we focused on the delicious meal again. After our plates were empty, we moved to the living room, where we all sat down on the various chairs and couches.

Travis yawned, bouncing Rose up and down on his leg.

"Let me cuddle this cutie," Kimberly exclaimed, taking the baby onto her lap.

"We've been sleeping on and off for the past few weeks," Bonnie said. "She's very active in the evening."

Travis yawned. "Very, very, *very* active. Thank God you and Reese are doing all the heavy lifting at the hotel, Kimberly. I can't wait for our new general manager to start in person."

Kimberly wrinkled her nose. "Yeah, I don't know about that. Maybe we made a mistake hiring him."

Their previous general manager left them in a lurch just last month. It had been a blow, especially considering the time of year. The new one had started already, but he was working remotely for now.

Travis shook his head. "He hasn't even arrived at the office. I can't believe you're ready to get rid of him."

"I'm not," Kimberly replied indignantly. "He's too full of himself. I don't like that." She rolled her eyes at Travis. "Stop giving me the evil eye. I won't run him off. He just needs to know what he's getting into."

"I think he's got a good idea," Reese said. Turning to me, she added, "Want to go get some wine?"

"Sure."

As she and I hunted for a bottle in the wine fridge in the kitchen, she said, "I think my sister actually likes our new guy."

"Ha! I had that impression too."

I bit back a laugh. Kimberly was such a spitfire. That morning, while we were following Lena's schedule, she'd kept bad-mouthing this guy—but then let it slip that he probably got away with all that self-importance because he was so good-looking.

Reese was definitely on to something.

"Time will tell, I guess. But my money is on some sparks flying between them soon." She picked a bottle of Maxwell chardonnay. "This one is a crowd favorite."

"It's delicious," I agreed. Tate certainly knew his business.

We uncorked the bottle before returning to the group and pouring wine for everyone.

"Let's toast to something fun," Kimberly suggested once everyone had a drink.

"To all our guys being in happy relationships with the greatest women, and to Kimberly and me, who will happily be the spinster aunts," Reese said.

"Oh, you two. That's no way to look at things," Beatrice said even as she raised her glass. "The right guys will come along. Like I always say, 'There are two things in life you don't have to chase: buses and men. The next one will be just around the corner.'"

To learn more about Layla Hagen & her books, visit laylahagen.com

Printed by Amazon Italia Logistica S.r.l.
Torrazza Piemonte (TO), Italy

63227777R00137